The Brandished Stars

THE CHILDREN OF THE GODS

MARTHELIZE DU TOIT

Copyright Case ID: 1-15040222051

LCCN: 2025924230

E-Book: 979-8-218-93168-1

Paperback: 979-8-218-93441-5

Hardcover: 978-1-291-82310-3

To all my closest friends. You know who you are. But mostly to my best friend, Carmien. I love you. Chase your dreams and never give up.

THE BRANDISHED STARS

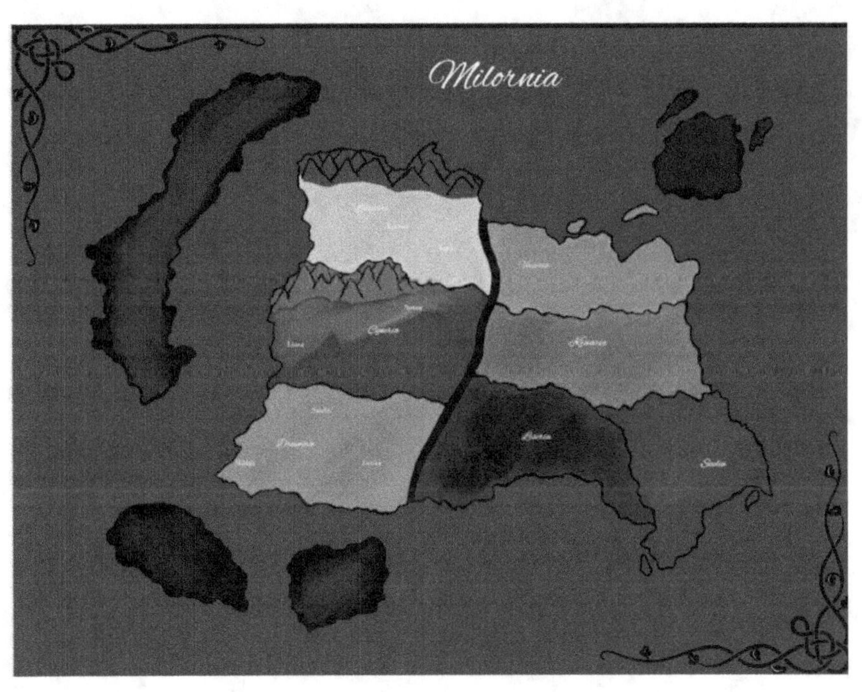

Milornia

Table of Contents

Part 1 viii

Chapter 1 1

Chapter 2 7

Chapter 3 15

Chapter 4 24

Chapter 5 32

Chapter 6 34

Chapter 7 45

Chapter 8 50

Chapter 9 52

Chapter 10 60

Chapter 11 65

Chapter 12 69

Chapter 13 77

Chapter 14 85

Chapter 15 91

Chapter 16 98

Chapter 17 103

Chapter 18 112

Chapter 19 116

Chapter 20 121

Chapter 21 134

Part 2 138

Chapter 22 139

Chapter 23 144

Chapter 24 152

Chapter 25 156

Chapter 26 159

Chapter 27 166

Chapter 28 169

Chapter 29 178

Chapter 30 189

Chapter 31 194

Chapter 32 200

Chapter 33 203

Chapter 34 215

Chapter 35 220

Chapter 36 226

Chapter 37 231

Chapter 38 238

Chapter 39 243

Chapter 40 249

Chapter 41 256

Acknowledgements 261

Part 1

Chapter 1

Valerie Denisera remembered two things: first, death had come to claim everyone she had loved. Second, she remembered the cold stone floor beneath her cheek. That was the last thing she could remember. Days bled together like seconds. Valerie wanted nothing more than to fade from the world. Night after night, she lay there. A knock on the door didn't stir her from the cold stone floor. She had a bed a few feet away, with lush white bedding and soft pillows. Her usual colourful cheeks were pale, her freckles standing out more against the pale shade. Her fingers curled around the nightgown clinging to her thigh. The sound of footsteps drew nearer. She fixed her eyes on a small crack on the bedroom wall, her eyes blurred, yet she refused to blink.

After listening for a few moments, she realized she had an audience. She didn't move her head; her eyes wandered to the feet that stood inches from her calf. She recognized the silver.

"Sleeping on the floor once more, Princess," the hoarse yet warm voice said. Finally, Valerie turned her head to look up at her friend's face. Commander Seraphina looked down at her friend curled up on the

1

floor. Without moving, she told the servants who had gathered to draw Valerie a bath to leave. After a few whispers, the three servant women flitted out of the room.

Valerie remained on the floor.

"I suppose I shouldn't call you Princess anymore," Sera said. Valerie couldn't even laugh at the attempt at humour. Slowly, she pushed herself up from the ground. Her neck and back were sore. Her brown curls fell around her face and down her back to the small space between her shoulder blades.

Sera always had a way of standing that made her seem bigger than she was. The silver armour sat snugly against her body, the morning light reflecting off the metal. Her belt hung on her hip, and the broadsword that lay there was untouched by dirt or grime. She must have cleaned it off before arriving.

Her friend looked her up and down but didn't speak. She knew better than to prod. Sera was one of the few people in the court who had never judged her or prescribed anything for her. She was friends with her because of that alone.

She took a moment to gaze at her friend. A new scar ran down the side of her face, from her cheekbone to the corner of her mouth. Her silver eyes remained fixed on Valerie as she moved to sit on the edge of her bed. Her black hair was cut short to her jawline and tied back, revealing her sharp cheekbones and fine mouth. Finally, after a few more moments of silence, Sera ventured a few words.

"How are you?" She always had a way of speaking that made Valerie drop all her walls in an instant. Tears burned her throat.

While her friend had been away on court errands, her mother had been assassinated in broad daylight, leaving Valerie to take the throne. Her hands bunched up in the sheets of the bed, and she bounced her knee; an anxious habit her mother had often tried to force her out of.

"Tired." The only thing she truly understood about her emotions. The first night after her mother's death, she had sat on the floor and stared at the wall. The second night, she had let a few tears slip. The third night, she curled up in her bed. Sleep had not found her for five days.

"Valerie, I'm so -"

Valerie cut her off with a stern look.

"Don't apologize," she rasped out.

"If I had been here, none of it would have happened. I could have…" Seraphina started taking a step forward, eyes fixed on the floor.

"Don't bring back the dead," Valerie uttered. Seraphina had often explained this to her after returning from missions where she had lost soldiers and been unable to protect innocents.

Valerie's eyes met hers, and an almost sad look passed in her friend's eyes. She moved to go, to give her space, but Valerie's hand reached out and grasped her friend's armoured hand. Seraphina turned to look at her, freezing where she stood.

"Stay." That was all Valerie could mutter without breaking into sobs. Seraphina merely sat down beside her. Valerie couldn't stop her mind from whirling. Her coronation was scheduled for the next day.

She felt bile rise in her throat. It had taken the servants over two hours to scrub her previous vomit from the bedsheets.

She didn't eat or sleep, yet she constantly felt the compulsion to retch. She curled into a ball with Seraphina by her side and wept.

Hours later, Valerie stood on a wooden box in the center of a lavish sitting room. Her arms were stretched out on either side of her body as the plump seamstress circled her with an artist's critical eye.

Jezebel had brown hair pulled back in a bun; she had plump cheeks and a mouth constantly pressed together in a grimace. She had fashioned many gowns for Valerie in the past, for balls and grand honorary celebrations.

And yet as Valerie stood there, pale and slightly dizzy, the woman did not attempt polite conversation, as if the thought of speaking to her was a frightening task. Her mother's death had not only thrown her into a state of numbness, but it had also elicited issues with the shipments of wool from their kingdom to the kingdom in the north and west. Very few servants or guards she knew attempted to speak with her, for fear she might blame her mother's untimely death on them.

Her advisors would deal with it. Upon her mother's sudden assassination, Valerie immediately passed on to her, who now had to deal with the three members, who had very different opinions on politics, grain, and wool.

A prickling sensation wrenched Valerie out of her thoughts.

"My apologies," Jezebel said, withdrawing the needle that had pricked her side. Although Valerie knew Jezebel was one of the most talented seamstresses in all the land, she dared not glance at the mirror that had been positioned directly in front of her. She had only known the colour of the fabric, a dark shade of blue, by looking down at herself once.

She could not bear to look in the mirror. She didn't know what she would find there. The seamstress withdrew a measuring tape from her small satchel and measured her bust, waist, and hips once more before giving a small, contented smile at her work.

"This might be one of my finest works," Jezebel said to herself. Only then did Valeria lift her head to the mirror. Her breath caught in her throat. It was the most beautiful piece of clothing she had ever seen.

The dark blue neckline dropped down to the valley between her breasts, accentuating their curve. The sleeves were tight towards the top, but slowly fanned out like feathers as they descended, the middle accentuating her waist, then curved over her hips, leaving her hands completely covered, with the sleeves reaching her thighs. The bodice cut down the middle, accentuating her waist and then curving over her hips, where a thin, golden embroidered piece sat. The skirts billowed out slightly, like water.

Valerie traced the delicate golden shapes that had been meticulously sewn into the fabric. It took her a moment to recognize the flowers that rimmed the bottom of the dress. She turned to examine the back, which fell low to the small of her spine.

She turned back to face the mirror,

"It's beautiful," Valerie said. Her voice sounded almost light. Jezebel curtsied politely.

"It is an honour, your majesty, truly."

With a slight nod, the woman helped her out of the dress to hang it up for the ceremony. She would be standing in front of the entire kingdom, accepting the crown her mother had once worn. She would be officially named the queen, and she would step into a position slightly lower than the gods.

Valerie could not say she believed in the gods.

She knew the faeries believed in gods. They had only a few, yet they believed in them so wholeheartedly that they were willing to die for them.

Her mother had died for less.

Once the seamstress had collected the dress and departed, a few servants flitted into the room. Valerie didn't miss the apprehensive glances exchanged among the servants, as if she were a caged animal to be approached with caution. The servants helped her back into her simpler white shirt, covered with a black vest and a matching skirt. The servants bowed quickly before disappearing.

She took a moment to glance at herself in the mirror once more. She saw her father in her face.

She had the same brow, the same button nose, the same dimples that rarely showed themselves in recent days.

Her mother's eyes stared back at her. Dark brown orbs seemed to mirror her dead mother.

She swallowed.

And without allowing herself to think further on her reflection, she turned away, leaving the mirror to stand there, chasing after her reflection. Which, day after day, seemed to become tainted.

Chapter 2

She nibbled on her dinner that night. Her advisors had wanted to speak to her at dinner about trivial matters, but she did not know specifically what they wanted to discuss.

Callus Hivrn on her right cleared his throat.

He had a pale complexion as if he had never seen the sunlight. Which he most likely hadn't. He was responsible for making sure all the kingdom's people were paying their dues and remaining content in their respective sectors throughout the kingdom. He spent his time in the library deep in the palace; he rarely came out.

"Your Majesty," he started, straightening himself and running a hand through his white beard for a moment.

"In recent months, after the…" he cut himself off, exchanging glances around the table. Valerie knew her advisors had liked her mother more than they had liked her, so they tiptoed around the fact that she was dead often.

"The people are under more pressure from the area surrounding the border. It seems that more merchants from Lunivere are crossing the border illegally."

One of the many laws her mother had found required that any human entering from Lunivere in the north or Dramira in the south be registered upon entry. Cyneria was known for its coal shipments, and if left unchecked, these smugglers would start importing and selling them at lower prices in larger quantities. Without strictly enforced border lines amongst the three human provinces and the four faerie kingdoms, there could be another war.

Only two great wars had passed between the faeries and humans. Both ended in so much loss that the ground still remembered the blood that had soaked it.

After a few moments of pondering, Valerie turned her attention to Callus.

"Can we send more soldiers to watch the borders along the north and south?" she asked, turning to the woman sitting across the table, Commander Arminia, who was responsible for all the troops Valerie had in her militia. "Can we send more soldiers to watch the borders along the north and south?" she asked. In turn, she turned to the woman sitting across the table, Commander Arminia, who was responsible for all the troops in Valerie's militia.

The woman had pitch-black hair and skin that was white in places from deep gashes on her face and throat. She had known her mother well and even considered her a friend.

She had more belief in Valerie on the throne than her mother had ever had in theory.

Her hazel eyes turned to Valerie, and she nodded slightly.

"About a third of our forces are distributed in the city and neighbouring towns, the other third is currently stationed on the borders."

"What about the remaining third?" Callus cut in. Arminia shot him a glance that held more ice than Valerie was used to. Yet again, she had consulted her advisors only twice in the past three months.

Before her coronation, she was still responsible for keeping the kingdom running. After her coronation, she would take full ownership and responsibility for all the laws, procedures, and executions of the sorcerers.

That was a thought she stuffed out of mind.

"The remaining third we are keeping in training. Since the conflicts with the faerie lands have been quiet in the past few years, we suspect that they may be plotting. A few of our best soldiers are currently sent as spies to get information. And considering the death of her majesty, we have invested in making sure the palace is ten times safer than it used to be."

Valerie felt her chest sting. Callus nodded his head, opening his mouth to speak once more, but with a small voice, Valerie interrupted.

"Excuse me, I must be retiring before the ceremony tomorrow," she said, standing as tall as she could without her legs buckling.

The trades advisor had muttered no words; he sat on her left, his eyes barely lifting as she stood. His black hair was combed back with gel. Dimitrius spoke rarely in general. Some days, Valerie wondered if he might be mute.

"Of course," Arminia said with a respectful dip of her head, which Valerie returned. Callus and Dimitrius bobbed their heads slightly in a sign of respect. With a gentle scraping of her chair, Valerie made her way to the double wooden doors on the side of the council room. She felt bile rising in her throat, and she stopped for a moment outside the council room to regain her carefully crafted composure.

Arminia had posted two guards to always stay near Valerie. Valerie had rarely spoken to either of the soldiers, one a tall man, no doubt a few years her senior, and a young woman who often cleared her throat. Both wore dark blue warrior garb. Armoured pieces crafted of dark blue sat on their chests, backs, and down to their ankles, built to withstand faerie magic to some extent. Their swords could cut through bones, faeries, and humans alike.

As Valerie walked, she thought of that fact alone.

Now that she was queen, she carried not only the power to decide how to rule, but also who to kill and who to spare.

From a young age, every human child was educated about Miloria's history. The faeries were placed on the earth by the gods themselves. For hundreds of years, they lived in harmony and peace, but as time took its toll, some of the faeries began to think more highly of themselves. The gods stripped themselves of their status and created humans, who wandered the earth for a much shorter time, stripped of their status. Their existence is merely to become a pest of sorts.

Compared to humans, faeries lived longer and possessed conduits, something that came straight from the gods.

Valerie tried to remember the lesson she had been taught by one of her history tutors over the years. Only when she reached her room and bid her guards a polite goodnight did she move to the bathing room. She sat there on the floor, staring at the ceiling.

Conduits, she remembered, were vessels the gods could inhabit. Because the faeries had become selfish and made themselves more than they were, the gods had removed themselves from their creation. They retreated to the heavens. However, nearly every faerie child born was a conduit for the gods. The gods controlled the faeries in that way, giving and taking power as they saw fit. For hundreds of years, the faeries and humans lived in harmony. Occasionally, there would be wars, but not to such an extent that the gods rained down thunder on Milornia and murdered all of them.

That was until the faeries started to enslave humans.

It all began when a faerie general, Colonius, took his sword in hand, raided a human village, and killed all the inhabitants. The human king was so furious that he had Colonius killed in turn.

That was the start of the First Great War.

The four faerie kingdoms tried to reason with humanity, but the humans were stubborn and would not tolerate any disrespect towards their people. Upon the arrival of one of the faerie lords, he was killed.

Days later, the remaining two faerie kingdoms marched on the human provinces. The slaughter that followed was the most horrific thing that had ever occurred. The faeries had taken Lunivere in the siege and had started to press in on Cyneria and Dramira. The humans who survived the siege of Lunivere were enslaved by the faeries, and for twenty years, that cycle continued.

Humans had lost nearly half of their population in the destruction of Lunivere. The conduits had overpowered them so easily that there had been no doubt that the humans were doomed.

Some humans were married to faeries, or they bore children by them. The offspring were half-human, half-faerie. There was one difference. A few of them were born as conduits. It seemed as if the gods were disgracing the union of the two races.

The sorcerers were on the cusp of two bloodlines, outcasts by the faeries for being half-human, and unable to return to Lunivere to rebuild their empire.

The two human kingdoms were beginning to buckle when the gods had compassion for their creation.

Throughout the human villages, conduits started to emerge. They remained hidden for years until they became soldiers.

It turned the tide of the war. The gods had scattered conduits amongst the humans.

During the First Great War, a woman arose unlike any before her. She had been chosen by the god of fire, one who burned hot with rage for both faeries and humans. She turned the tide of the war, wiping out thousands of faeries that commanded Lunivere. She took the throne for herself and ruled the humans for a short time. Most of the conduit warriors who were sorcerers were suddenly wanted. The faeries and the humans began fighting over who should have the warriors. But the few conduits that remained disappeared from society; some rumoured that the gods had taken back their powers, while others claimed they had all died.

After Lunivere was restored to a human king, the gods repaid the evil the faeries had committed, thereby preventing some children from being born as conduits. The human conduits were then integrated into the sorcerer's population.

As Valerie sat there, she had always wondered why the conduits had disappeared. She knew they had no doubt loathed to be fought over, but without their powers, what were they?

Her stomach churned again.

After the Second Great War, the massacres and deaths of human royal families and unspeakable brutalities, the border was built. Where bridges or canyons separated the three human borders, the border with the faerie lands was the largest ever made. Her father had fought in that war, the war that had ended merely one hundred years prior. He had been nothing but a boy prince, yearning to prove something to his father.

The war had been brutal. Thousands of human innocents caught in the crossfire, faerie children abducted and slaughtered.

It had been horrific for humans, faeries, and sorcerers.

After her grandfather died on the front lines in the Second Great War, her father took the throne. As he grew into a young man, the boy king corresponded and formed a three-way alliance.

Shortly after her parents were wed, the wall was built.

In total, it had taken three years to complete the wall. It stood at over one hundred feet tall and was sixty feet wide, spanning from the southern tip of Milornia up into the mountains of Lunivere. There was no way to cross the border except by scaling the wall. Each province was responsible for stationing as many soldiers as possible on the wall to provide continuous surveillance.

Her father had died one day at the border.

She knew not the day he had died, other than the fact that her mother had wept, and until the day she had died, she had lost a piece of herself.

Her father had believed that the faeries could be trusted. It had cost him his life.

Her mother had told her that she could not be as foolish a ruler as her father had been. Her mother had gone from a quiet queen to a warrior who killed all sorcerers she could get her hands on within their borders.

Her rage for the half-breed children of faeries had led to a slaughter that went unquestioned. Valerie had seen so many executions in her life that she knew how people died. Knew they could be hanged or beheaded, boiled or tortured.

It usually mattered how her mother felt on the chosen day.

She had seen women and children slaughtered simply because of the blood that flowed in their veins.

Bile rose again, and she bent over the porcelain basin, squeezing her eyes shut as tightly as she could, her head throbbing. She would be responsible for overseeing every execution. The thought made her head spin.

She had never had the chance to speak to a sorcerer or a faerie. When she was a child, she had wanted nothing more than to make friends with them.

Now she wanted nothing more than to crawl under the covers of her bed and stay there until she withered.

She rose slowly from the floor and looked in the mirror. She examined her features as a painter might observe their canvas. She took in every inch of her face, every curl that framed it.

She could feel the raw terror in her chest. The fear that she would not feel anything towards the dead. But she remembered her mother's cold voice as if she stood there with her.

They are an abomination, and they slaughtered your father like cattle. We have every right to hate them.

Valerie clutched the counter. She had never known genuine hatred, never felt blood on her skin or fear that ate away at her soul, but she knew that her mother's rage would no doubt bleed into her own if she did not control it.

She would become a monster in time. She knew that.

And yet as she trudged back to her room, mouth tasting like ash as she slid under the covers, she clung to the hope that she would not become her mother. That the monster would pass over her.

But she knew that the next day, when she knelt before the high priestess and accepted the crown her father had borne, she was only accepting the doom that would find her more swiftly than her hatred for her blood.

Chapter 3

Breathing felt like an impossible feat as Valerie slipped into the dress. Jezebel had arrived early in the afternoon. The seamstress helped her into the dress, and yet it felt as if it were nothing more than a vice around her body.

Her stomach was filled with knots, and her face was slightly flushed from the anxious feeling clawing at her throat.

The two servants who usually attended to her bustled around the room as Jezebel ordered them around in almost a militaristic fashion, bringing over necklace after necklace that the seamstress pressed gently to her throat, looked at for a moment, and then asked for another.

Valerie felt as if she were a doll to be dressed. Her hands fidgeted with the inside of her sleeves as she waited for the seamstress to deem her ready.

The entire kingdom would be at the coronation. She felt her heart launch into her throat at the thought. She had only ever once been paraded around, only a few days old, swaddled against her mother's chest.

This was a completely different spectacle.

On occasion, she would appear when her mother made announcements to the kingdom, a rarity in itself. Valerie had spent most of her life sheltered in the palace, surrounded by tutors and scholars, learning about trade, battle, theory, and ethics; everything she would need to lead the kingdom into war, if need be.

Her mother had possessed very little faith that she would be a good ruler, and she made sure that she was painfully aware of it.

As Valerie stepped down from the small box, the seamstress examined her work, while a servant ensured her curls tumbled down her back just right.

All the lessons her tutors had taught her seemed utterly useless in that moment, as if they were worth nothing.

Knowing how to fight a war was very different from governing a kingdom.

Over the past few days, she had been informed of the King and Queen of Dramira, who wanted to have a meeting with her in due time. She had never met the King and Queen, but rumour had it they were as calm as the Oceanside that bordered their land. Rarely get into arguments and are generally considered to be practically perfect rulers.

The South was known for its rich culture, diverse foods, and distinctive dialects. Some rumoured that most of the inhabitants had sailed to Dramira from a faraway continent. Valerie had always wanted to know what it felt like to have the sea air in her nose, the wind whipping through her hair as she went everywhere, anywhere but her throne.

"You look stunning, Your Majesty," Jezebel bowed in a low reverence, and Valerie nodded respectfully before the servants followed the seamstress out of the room. Valerie was left alone with her thoughts as she looked in the mirror.

The woman who stared back at her looked so different that she almost gasped. Her hair fell in dark brown curls down her back, and her brown eyes were made to look brighter with perfectly placed cosmetics. A silver necklace fell down her neck to rest just above the valley of her chest. Her mouth was its natural pink shade, and she resisted the urge to bite her lip.

The door opened, and Valerie didn't need to turn to find out who it was.

Seraphina stopped a few feet away, smiling almost sadly. She wore her standard silver armour. Where the palace guards wore blue to be easily distinguished from other soldiers, her friend wore traditional military armour. The silver reflected the sun.

She would escort her to the ceremony. "Do I look alright?" Valerie asked.

She had never cared much about her appearance, but that day was likely the most important day of her life.

"You look like Queen Val," Seraphina said lightly. She tried not to cringe at the word "queen." The word sounded sour.

She knew what being queen would make her into—a murderer.

"Are you ready?" Seraphina asked, and Valerie turned from the mirror to meet her friend's eyes, forcing a small smile.

"As ready as I'll ever be," she said, and Seraphina stepped aside as Valerie lifted her dress and made her way towards the door. The mirror showed her the last reflection of herself as a princess, a girl in a sense. The next time Valerie gazed in the mirror, it would be a very different reflection staring back.

The royal carriage awaited them. Valerie stepped into the lavish space. Seraphina and the other guards flanking the carriage were to walk beside it, watching for threats. Valerie was left with her thoughts, fidgeting with her skirts.

She gazed out the carriage window as the path from the palace wound down the hill towards the town. She sat there, staring out at the green forests, with hawks screeching above and deer grazing between the trees.

The town of Linra was a sight to behold.

The usually quiet streets were teeming with people, cheering at the sight of the carriage. Her stomach twisted painfully. Children were hoisted on their parents' shoulders, waving small blue handkerchiefs, the kingdom's national colour. She felt bile rise in her throat.

She would be a queen to her people, but a murderer of hundreds, even thousands, of sorcerers. She had no choice. If she chose not to kill, the other two nations would turn on her kingdom. If she did, blood would soak her skin, yet her kingdom would survive at least until she was replaced. As soon as she accepted the crown her people were cheering for, she would be seen as a weapon of the dead. Of her mother.

The cheering grew louder as they moved deeper into the town. The city's architecture was unlike that of any other city in Cyneria. The white pillars rose high into the sky, slopes formed doorways, and stone steps formed passageways that cut into sharp, cold alleys. From the windows, towels and pieces of clothing hung. The carriage continued its slow pace through the city, heading for the Pathagrius, their destination.

The cliff on which all kings and queens of Cyneria had been crowned. The building that stood there was the most beautifully sculpted, except for the palace. Its roof stretched a hundred feet into the air, supported by white pillars that held up the circular space. The domed ceiling allowed light to cast an almost ethereal brightness across the Pathagrius. Valerie had seen it only once in her life. She had stood in black gowns beside her mother as her father was sent to a peaceful rest with the gods before being burnt to ashes by the cliffs and scattered in the water below.

The city of Linra bordered the ocean, and unlike the kingdom of Dramira, which was built against the cliffside, it gazed out at the sea, never touching it.

Her stomach tied into knots once more as they reached the cobblestone path that made its way up the cliff. She spotted the structure out the window, and she felt the urgent need to retch as they finally slowed to a stop. The civilians would be allowed to wait outside the Pathagrius to congratulate her as she made her first appearance as Queen.

Guards - wearing silver - had stationed themselves along either side of the pathway as the carriage slowed to a stop. Her stomach launched into her throat as she tried to steady her breathing. The door opened, and the sunlight filtered in. She took a moment to steady herself as she took her first step out of the carriage onto the cobblestone. The sun was high in the sky, and clouds were scattered perfectly as if it were a canvas.

The people cheered from where they stood off the path, clustered on the grass. She graced a small smile, not waving as she held herself upright, turning from the carriage and setting her gaze on the Pathagrius.

She swallowed, her skin clammy under the dress as she slowly ascended the white stone steps. Seraphina gave her a slight nod as she took her station at the sloped entrance. It was so silent inside the Pathagrius that she could hear her heart beating in her ears.

The space was nearly empty save for the royal priestess standing at the center of the room on a pedestal. Valerie forced herself to meet her gaze, even though it made her skin crawl.

The Priestesses of Cyneria had been part of their history since humans first graced Milornia. They were the only people in the human world who truly believed in the gods. They wore dark red robes, which gave them an almost sinister appearance. Each priestess was brought into power by the high priestess, who chose her lieges. They remained cut off from Linra, living far off in the mountains that bordered Lunivere, appearing in Cyneria only for royal births, deaths, or coronations.

Valerie stopped short of the pedestal.

The high priestess let a small smile grace her lips as she gazed down at Valerie. Her eyes softened slightly, those green orbs strangely deep. Her white hair was covered

with a hood that veiled most of her face. The only distinguishing feature between her and the young priestess who stood beside her was the black stripe that ran from her lower lip down under her cape.

The younger woman held a plush pillow on the sofa. Her vision blurred for a moment.

She had seen the crown so many times in her life, traced every pattern on its side while sitting in her father's lap. But with it sitting there, waiting almost - it sent a chill down Valerie's stomach.

Whether the priestess recognized the expression on her face or not, she didn't show any sign of recognition.

She cleared her throat once, forcing Valerie to look at the woman.

"Kings and Queens have come and gone from this world; they have instilled war and peace, suffering and safety." While she spoke, Valerie looked towards her outstretched hands. She hesitated before placing her hands in the woman's. It was like touching ice.

Valerie resisted the urge to yank her hands away.

"As Queen, you will rule with strength, wisdom, and…"

The Priestess paused.

It was common knowledge that the high priestesses received visions from the gods; they could see whether the royal would be a good or bad leader. The look in the woman's eyes sent a surge of panic through Valerie's heart.

"Unspeakable power."

The woman met her eyes, and Valerie swore she could see fear there. But it went so quickly that she thought she must have seen things.

The woman released Valerie's hands and reached for the crown on top of the pillow.

"Heir of Greyson and Adina, I now crown you Valerie Denisera, Queen of Cyneria, until you part from this world, or another succeeds you." With those words, Valerie bowed her head and accepted the crown.

It sat heavily on her curls, and she had to straighten her neck to keep it on her head.

She raised her head, and the priestess had donned a bowl, the contents of which

Valerie did not know.

The woman smudged her finger along the inside, then raised her hand with a blackened finger to Valerie's head, drawing a symbol on the center of her forehead—a circle with a line through it, both diagonally and vertically.

Every priestess bowed reverently as Valerie started her walk back to the entrance of the Pathagrius. Her head throbbed, and she forced her lip to stop quivering. The woman had looked so frightened upon speaking of her reign. She assumed it was because she would be slaughtering sorcerers and faeries for however long it took her to pass into the afterlife.

As she walked, she stepped into the sunlight. The crowds stilled for a moment, then one by one they dropped to their knees before her. She felt all the air in her lungs leave as everyone, including her guards, knelt before her. She swallowed thickly as she walked down the steps, and slowly everyone rose to their feet and cheered.

Her knees threatened to buckle under the weight of the crown, finally settling on her shoulders. She could not meet Seraphina's eyes as Seraphina flanked her right. She strolled down the steps, forcing a smile as she slowly climbed into the carriage. Her stomach churned so violently that she had to grip the plush settee, her eyes closed.

She didn't hear the cheering that grew like booms of thunder outside the carriage.

She didn't feel anything except for the fear that coiled deep in her chest.

She didn't remember arriving back at the palace or the servants who bowed low.

Valerie only remembered stumbling into her bathroom and vomiting into the porcelain bowl. Her knees buckled fully, and she collapsed to the ground, clinging to the porcelain bowl as bile rose in her throat. She retched for a few minutes. After the nausea seemed to pass, she sat back slightly against the wall, still within reach of the bowl if the need arose.

Sweat clung to her forehead, and she took deep, shaky breaths. With shaky fingers, she reached up and removed the crown from her head. She held it in her hands, and she could almost feel her father's hand brushing a curl from her face. Could hear the soft timber of his voice and see the blue eyes that always made her feel safe.

Valerie had the sudden, consuming urge to throw the crown across the room.

Her father had always believed she would make a good queen. From a young age, he had treated her in such a way that she had never, for a second, doubted herself. Then he had died, and with him the last faith in her being a good queen. Her mother had forced her to study endlessly since she was nine years old, poring over old war manuscripts and official laws crafted with pristine care. She had learned various languages, had mastered nearly every dance form, and had learned how to appear beautiful in the face of courtiers.

Valerie had never been accepted. From the moment her mother took the throne, she had been poked, prodded, and shaped into a distorted version of her mother. She gripped the crown so hard that its pointed top dug into her palms.

She felt the urge to cry.

Tears burned hot in her throat, but she forced herself to gaze upwards at the ceiling to avoid the feeling. If she started to cry now, she would never stop. She was the sole heir of Cyneria, and if she became weak, then the kingdom would buckle. She despised her mother; she wanted nothing more than to shatter the crown and let one of her advisors take the throne. But there was no other.

She would be despised and ostracized by society.

And yet something within her wouldn't allow her father's house to be defiled. Wouldn't allow her father to turn in his grave because of her insolence. If she were to be a monster, then she would be.

Valerie had never been naive in her life. Because even in that bathing room, the gods listened.

Chapter 4

Within two days of her coronation, Valerie had been moved to the royal bedroom. Its bed is three times the size of her old one, and the closet is almost as large as the kitchen. Jezebel and a few of her trusted maids had taken great care in creating an entirely new wardrobe for Valerie. Colours, gauzes, sashes, and silks were thrown in her old bedroom. Between meetings with her advisors, she found herself perched on the wooden stage being poked and prodded.

Her advisors had been providing her with constant reports on their duties. Arminia had left to survey the soldiers at the border and train the recruits. She received no news, save for the occasional letter that Seraphina would read in her stead. Her friend was directly under Arminia and was therefore entrusted with making decisions on her behalf. Callus focused constantly on the influx of trade between the north and south, and on whether her coronation had affected the average tax the citizens of Cyneria paid.

The King and Queen of Lunivere were to arrive in Cyneria in the coming days for formal meetings about trade. While the Cyneria mountains could offer coal, the Dramira oceans could offer pearls, diamonds, and rare jewels of great value. Without them, there would be very few nice things in Cyneria. Callus focused on arranging preparations once they arrived. Without the jewels, he would lose so much silver that Valerie would get rid of him.

Valerie found herself already pulled in multiple directions. As queen, she was now responsible for numerous aspects of their kingdom. She received news from her three advisors nearly every day.

It wasn't until around a week into her rule that Dimitrius finally spoke.

Valerie had been sitting in her new study, one that her mother had spent a lot of time in. Her hand was gripping a pen, scribbling on a blank sheet of paper. The knock on the door was abrupt.

Over the years, she had grown accustomed to seeing Dimitrius inside the palace; he often lingered about and was only visible when he was dealing with her mother. The door opened, and he stepped inside.

Valerie looked up. Her tired eyes latched onto his face.

"Propositions for your courting have arrived, your majesty."

Valerie was both taken aback by his speaking and by the meaning of his words. He walked to the desk, and she hid her hands so he wouldn't notice the black ink stains on her palms.

"The Prince of Dramira has expressed his desire to court you," Dimitrius said, setting down a formal letter from the prince. Valerie glanced over it, too tired to form words properly.

"I have not been ruling for a month," she said, almost shocked that marriage was already a consideration.

"Exactly, Prince Castiler finds it impertinent that you two are wed." Valerie looked at him for a moment, then she sighed. She tightened her hand in her lap. Marriage had been something her mother had never wanted to resort to. She had firmly believed that Valerie should learn how to be a queen on her own, and then one day produce an heir. Not the other way around.

Just as Valerie opened her mouth to respond, a knock sounded on the door.

Dimitrius let out a frustrated breath, biting his cheek.

Seraphina stepped inside. She looked towards Dimitrius and bowed her head slightly before she turned to Valerie. The look in Seraphina's eyes made Valerie tense with fear. Her friend was very rarely this pale.

"What is it?" Valerie asked, now completely forgetting the advisor who still lingered.

"We've found one, your majesty," Seraphina said in a voice almost a whisper.

"What?" Valerie asked, feeling her heart launch in her chest, it could be anything, a report from Arminia stating that war had begun, that faeries were marching on the city -

"A sorcerer, your majesty."

The world faded for a moment. Valerie had tried to avoid thinking about the fact that she was to kill sorcerers, according to the law. A law that no one would ever let her change unless she challenged her advisors. Valerie was in no mood for them.

"Where are they?" Valerie asked, standing already. She knew what she had to do.

"In the town square," the words sent Valerie clutching the table. They would wait there until she arrived to finish the job or at least give them the order.

"Take me to them," she said, turning to Seraphina, who gave her an almost sad look. She bid Dimitrius farewell and tried not to retch as Seraphina led her to the carriage.

When they arrived at the town square, guards kept the crowds back. Those who had cheered for her now spat at the sorcerer kneeling on the ground. Valerie stepped out of her carriage, feeling dread and guilt. The prisoners had their heads covered with sacks, their hands tied behind their backs. Seraphina walked forward and grasped the man by the arm, hauling him to his feet as if he were a child. Her stomach tied itself into so many knots she swore she couldn't feel her hands.

The man wasn't pleading; he stood and didn't dare struggle against Seraphina's hold. She had enough strength to snap his arm in her grip if she wanted to. Her friend's eyes remained trained on her face.

She looked regal.

Her dark green dress trailed behind her as she took a step, then another. Her hair fell in loose curls down her back, and to the naked eye, she looked as strong as she had been days before. Yet as Valerie stood there, she never felt more like a child.

She had never killed. She had watched as soldiers returned, as if they had done something horrible, something they could not speak of. She had always wondered what that felt like; now she would.

This was to be her first kill, the first of thousands.

She wanted nothing more than to abolish the law, but if she did, she risked undermining the already strained alliances with the other kingdoms. She took another step forward. The center of the square had been set up with a block. Seraphina tugged the man towards the wooden box. The palace executioner stood to the side of it, axe in hand. He could sever the man's head so cleanly that the man wouldn't know he was dead. All the citizens went quiet as Valerie stepped forward until she was nearly in front of the block. Bile rose in her throat, and she had to count in her head to slow her breathing. Her heart thundered in her ears and chest. She felt as if she couldn't breathe. As if it were impossible.

The man grunted as his knees hit the cobblestone. Then he said a word. "Please."

Valerie felt her heart stop for a singular moment. She knew that voice, having heard it in the palace before. She turned to Seraphina, who stood with her hand on the back of the man's neck to hold him upright.

"Take off the sack," she said. At the sound of her voice, the man stiffened; he didn't speak. The executioner turned to her, his black hair shorn close to his head, eyes cold.

"But Your Majesty, he is a sorcerer, he is filthy," the executioner said. Valerie forced herself to speak again.

"He will die anyway. I would like to see his face."

At her expressing a wanting to see a sorcerer's face, the crowd let out an audible gasp. Sorcerers were beautiful creatures, half human, half faerie. They didn't live half as long as faeries, but she needed to see him. Because if she were imagining his voice, then everything would be alright.

The sack was ripped from his head, and Valerie nearly gasped. General Ladib looked up at her. His green eyes widened in shock at the sight of her, and he tried to get up, only to have Seraphina's hand clamp down harder on the back of his neck. His hair fell to his shoulders, but it was the same face as her father's military commander, the same face she had seen at the dinner table all those years ago.

"I thought you were dead," Valerie dared. The crowd murmured at her words, no doubt shocked to see the general kneeling, beheaded. He shook his head, almost sorrowfully. He had been there the day her father died, standing on the wall as her father was shot with arrows. A sudden rage filled Valerie. Her brow creased as she looked down at the general, who now appeared to be shaking.

"I'm sorry," he said.

But someone screamed at him from the crowd. "Scum."

The crowd started to roar again. Valerie had loved him when she was a little girl and had always flocked to him when he returned from the war with her father. Had called

Uncle Lad always hugged him tightly around the neck. Here he knelt on the ground—a traitor.

She hadn't known he was a sorcerer. Executions that were carried out in the town square were for sorcerers and faeries. The ones done in the dungeon were for traitors to the crown. She wanted nothing more in that moment than to say it wasn't fair. But she knew she couldn't. She had suspected him dead after he hadn't returned with her father's patrol guard.

Rumours had spread that the general had murdered her father; now it seemed even more true. But he wouldn't be tried or tested. He would be killed.

Her stomach roiled, and she squeezed her eyes shut. Seraphina put his head down on the block. He didn't cry; he knew better than to. The executioner lifted his axe high in the air. Valerie felt dread deep inside her chest as she met the general's eyes once more.

Seraphina spoke.

"You are hereby sentenced to die, General Ladib, under the law of old."

The crowd still for a moment, and it felt as if the air cleaved open when the axe swung down and landed with a sickening crunch.

The sun had long since gone down as Valerie sat in her room. However, it didn't feel like hers. The candle on the table had melted halfway since she had lit the wick, and her hands shook slightly as she reread the report.

Papers were scattered across her desk, and she sat there in her white nightgown, rereading her father's death report. After he had died, the last remaining soldiers of his legion had confirmed his death and that of the rest of those lost. She read one part six times.

General Ladib, death unknown.

She threw the paper down on the desk and ran a hand over her face. She hadn't been able to sleep. Upon returning to the palace, she had lain on the floor in the bathing room for hours, until Seraphina came to coax her downstairs for dinner. She had taken two bites and then returned to her room.

Servants who stood outside her door had been ordered to retrieve the archive scrolls from the library and had returned with arms full. Almost thirty different soldiers in her father's legion had claimed the general hadn't died, or at least his body hadn't been found.

If he had been killed earlier that day, then he was no doubt a sorcerer. Had her mother known this? Had she hunted for him and, in doing so, slaughtered thousands? She clenched her hands tightly, her nails digging crescent moons into her skin. She couldn't sleep. If she did, she would wake up, and nothing would have changed. Staying awake provided control. A peace in knowing exactly what would follow her. In sleep, she could not determine the dreams that plagued her.

She set the scroll down. Told herself she would sleep for a little while. The dawn would soon awaken her. She lay her head on the desk, her eyes fluttering closed.

Little did she know what awaited her in the dark.

31

Chapter 5

Darkness filled the bedroom as Valerie blew out her candle. It was not the kind of darkness brought on by the lack of light. It was the kind of darkness that maimed and killed.

The gods gazed down at Valerie asleep, unaware of the thing watching her in her sleep. It took its form slowly, as if unwinding itself. The figure stood in the shape of a woman, her midnight-black hair cascading down her back, her face pale, her eyes cold. The goddess of death rarely traversed the world. The other gods took more pleasure in walking amongst their people as they saw fit, but seldom.

She ran a pale finger over the desk, her black skirt swishing at her ankles. She knew this girl was the queen. But she had not yet picked a conduit, not since the one before her had perished.

The goddess smiled an almost crude smile as she gazed down at the girl. Without giving a moment's notice, she placed a hand flat on the girl's back.

The goddess was not a cruel entity. She had seen visions of this girl before, of what she would do. The goddess smiled softly, then leaned down to brush the girl's ear with her mouth, as shadows curled and uncurled around their master.

"You are mine."

The goddess whispered in her ear, and before she even stood, she vanished from this world and stepped into the next. Valerie would not know why it had happened.

That night, as she lay curled on her desk, the shadows awaited her at the beck and call of the shadows, like waiting watchdogs eager to please their owner.

Chapter 6

Valerie awoke to the sound of rustling. Her head throbbed, and she felt as though she had swallowed a rock. Her dream had not been kind; she had seen General Ladib being slaughtered repeatedly. She sat up as she heard more shuffling. One of the young servant girls she had now grown used to seeing in the morning flitted around the room. Upon seeing Valerie awake, the servant girl bowed low.

"Your Highness," she said, making her way over to Valerie, who rubbed her eyes clean of sleep.

"Shall I take these for you?" she asked, gesturing to the table scattered with scrolls. Valerie lifted her head, shaking it firmly.

"No, it's alright," she said, and began gathering the scrolls on top of each other. Her head pounded, and she felt a nagging sensation deep in her gut. She paid it no mind as she made her way to the bathing room. After washing her face, she returned to her room.

The servant girl had a strange complexion. Her face had white spots, even though her skin was a dark brown. To Valerie, she looked like a beautiful canvas. The room was warm, and sunlight streamed in as the girl pulled back the heavy red curtains. The sound of waves crashing in the distance and gulls screeching above filled the air as the window opened.

The girl had been seen around the palace for a few months, and her mother had insisted that new servants be brought in.

The ocean draft blew the white curtains away from the windows, and for a moment, Valerie was a little girl again, standing in this very room with her father, gazing out at the ocean. When she had been naive enough to believe forsaking the crown was possible, she had wished for a way to explore the oceans, the vast expanse of sea, and never returned.

The crown held her down now.

"General Seraphina has requested to see you in the war room this morning," the girl said softly, as if she were afraid to disturb Valerie from her daydreams. Her eyes softened as she turned to the girl.

"Did she say why?"

"No, Your Highness."

Valerie clenched her jaw. Seraphina never summoned her; if she had, it must be something serious. Without removing her eyes from the now open window, she let her hands wring together.

"Please tell her I will be with her shortly," Valerie said softly, as if unsure of her decision. The servant girl didn't seem to notice it as she bowed low.

"Of course, Your Majesty," the girl left the room as swiftly as she had come, white skirt twirling around her ankles.

Valerie had grown tired of being referred to as "Your Majesty" or "Your Highness." Before her crowning, people had addressed her by name; now she was nothing more than a monarch.

When two servant girls came to her room to help her get dressed, she allowed them to strip her out of her nightgown. Before she knew it, she was dressed in a deep green dress with a high slit on the right thigh. There was no crown on her head when she gazed at the mirror. But she swore she could see a flicker of something before she turned her head away.

Seraphina stood at the long table in the center of the room when Valerie entered. She bowed low as anyone might, and when their eyes met, Valerie knew something had happened.

"What is it?" She asked, still aware that her voice was rougher than it would usually be, still heavy with sleep. The guards stationed around the room watched as Seraphina pulled a scroll from where she had left it on the table.

Valerie stood across from her, separated by a few feet from her friend. The scroll unfurling was the only sound for a few terse moments, and then Seraphina cleared her throat. When she spoke, it was a commander's voice.

"The recent reports of the border have fluctuated in the past few weeks. At first, I assumed there was nothing of importance, but reports of scouts on the wall have been more recent."

The words cut through the air as Seraphina pointed to the map laid out in front of them. The massive wall that split the faerie lands from the mortal lands had small red dots drawn on it.

"These are where sightings have occurred," Seraphina said, pointing to the dots on the border.

It was not uncommon for patrols to catch sight of some faerie scouts on occasion, but concerning General Ladib's death, and the stillness that had fallen since her mother's death, it could be more than a common occurrence.

Valerie found her mind spinning. She had spent countless hours with military tutors, observing strategy and defensive plans. Her head spun slightly as she forced her mind to clear. Every time she blinked, she saw the General's head lolling on the ground.

"How many scouts?"

"On our portion of the border, only three, but reports from Lunivere and commanders say at least five on each of their borders."

Valerie sucked in a sharp breath. The faerie lands had been quiet for months; her mother had formed mutualistic alliances between the other human kingdoms, and the three military generals often clashed about the border.

"How many soldiers do we have stationed on the borders between Lunivere and Dramira?" Valerie asked, observing the map as she had done a hundred times before with her tutors.

"On the western border, we have fifty, and roughly the same amount on the eastern border."

"How many on the wall?"

"Since our last reports came in, we have almost one hundred soldiers stationed on the border from morning to evening, with rotations, of course," Seraphina said. In that moment, Valerie understood why she was a general. She could command armies and yet be her friend while doing so. Valerie lifted her hand from the map, her hands finding purchase in her skirt.

"How many are here in the kingdom?" "Roughly five thousand."

The number sent Valerie losing a tight breath. Her mother had enlisted thousands of new soldiers from across Cyneria in hopes of building a larger arsenal should the foreign lands retaliate. But five thousand-

The number seemed so large that it took Valerie a moment to respond appropriately. One thing was sure: they needed to prepare because the faerie kingdoms would soon start something. And Valerie wasn't sure she could win a war.

By the time Valerie finished her meeting with Seraphina, a servant had come to announce the arrival of the King and Queen of Lunivere. Their arrival had been delayed by political tensions that had flared in their lands over the faeries at their border. Unlike the faeries seen at the Cynerian border, more attempts to infiltrate the kingdom had occurred.

Valerie had assumed it would take a lot longer for them to make their way to Cyneria, finally. The servants waiting in her bedroom had rapidly fixed her hair, brought her crown, which was quickly placed on her head, before Seraphina escorted her to the throne room.

Unlike the other rooms in the palace, which were constantly cleaned and rearranged, the throne room was kept in pristine condition and reserved only for annual balls, such as her coronation ball, which took days to prepare. When she reached the throne room, the king and queen awaited her patiently, standing before her throne. Upon seeing her, they knelt.

Valerie had only seen the King and Queen of Lunivere once before, in a meeting with her mother a few months ago. Upon hearing the news earlier and upon hearing of her death, the King and Queen sent their condolences. They hadn't changed in the slightest.

"Rise," Valerie said as she climbed the stairs to her throne and watched as the king and queen rose. King Ladian rose with dark brown hair that fell in gangly strands to the sides of his face, and he did not have his crown on his head. Both the king and queen wore their thick fur coats, and Valerie had the urge to offer them something more extraordinary to wear. Cyneria was constantly bombarded by heat; they must be melting under all those furs.

The king's face was graced with a soft smile as his wife rose beside him.

Queen Nira always wore a look that made people feel comfortable in her presence. She had black curls braided down her back, her fur coat covering the neckline of her dress, yet still allowing her skirts to flow around her ankles.

"We are truly sorry we could not arrive for your coronation," she said, her voice airy and light. Valerie noticed how her hand rested slightly on her belly, and her eyes softened ever so slightly. She didn't move to sit down on her throne; instead, she walked down the steps and stood a few feet away from the king and queen.

"It is not a problem," Valerie said politely, looking from Ladian to his wife, "all that matters is that you are here now." She said with as much gentleness as she could muster. Her mind was still swimming with thoughts concerning the wall, her mother's death, and her coronation. She felt a sudden flood of exhaustion so heavy she had to force herself to focus on the royals.

"I will have a room prepared for you. Feel free to stay as long as you like," she said, her voice holding gentleness. The queen was about to open her mouth to say something when a servant rushed to Valerie's side, bowing to the royals before making her way to Valerie's side instantly.

"Your Majesties," she said, then turned to Valerie in waiting. The queen was silent but did not seem offended. Valerie bowed slightly in apology for the interruption before turning to the servant.

"What is it?"

"More sorcerers have been found; they are in the dungeon as we speak."

The words sent a chill down her spine, and for a moment, she couldn't breathe. Her hands shook, and she fisted them in her skirt before she turned to the servant again.

"Can it wait?" Valerie asked, her eyes flicking back to the king and queen, who had started to converse.

"No, Your Majesty, there are children involved."

The words sent bile flaring in her throat. She hated the words that had just been uttered. She felt her mind go blank. How would she deal with a child sorcerer? Would they have to be killed alongside their parents? The thought in itself sent her feet feeling numb.

She turned away from the servant with a precision so like her mother's.

"Your Graces, I must excuse myself from your presence; my servant here will escort you to your room for the duration of your time here in Cyneria," she said, and the queen smiled warmly at her husband and then at Valerie before the servant led them away.

Her stomach didn't stop churning as she made her way to the dungeon. The only time her guards imprisoned sorcerers was if they had committed treason. She hated how her mother's voice filled her head as she approached the dungeon.

You are not a priestess or a saint; do not mourn for those undeserving of mercy.

The dungeon reeked of death.

Valerie should have turned around then and retreated to her room. But she could not, when everyone knew what she had to do. Keep them safe. In previous years, she had doubted her mother's ruthlessness and wondered if murdering sorcerers was the right solution.

And now-

Now she realized that her advisors would never allow her to stop killing. They wanted safety, and the only way to give them that would be to kill for them. Her hands shook as she followed another guard. She was shorter than Seraphina, with auburn hair tied back from a freckled face. Her mind was spinning as they finally reached the small cell. She knew what she would behold when she gazed inside, but that didn't stop the bile that rose in her throat.

The woman sat there on the ground holding a small babe to her chest. Her eyes were red and bloodshot as if she had been crying for hours. The baby fussed against her mother's chest, and Valerie felt her throat tighten as she gazed at the baby's face.

"What are they charged for?" Valerie asked the female guard who now stood at the side of the cell, her hand on her sword at her hip.

"The woman is a sorcerer, Your Majesty. They were found smuggling bread in the market."

At that, the woman let out a cry.

"No, Your Majesty. Please, my baby and I are starving," she said, her eyes filling with tears instantly. She stood, legs shaky, approaching the cell to beg, but the female guard turned swiftly, hand on her sword. The woman glanced at the sword and let out a broken sob immediately.

"Please," the woman begged, her hands cradling her babe to her chest.

The dread that flooded Valerie at that moment was so heavy that for a moment, it felt as if she was watching the scene from a distance. Her nails dug into her palm as she beheld the woman and her newborn babe. If the mother were killed, then her baby would be taken, and she would most likely die. Her mother had killed hundreds of women like this one. How was this treason?

Her throat burned with tears, but she did not allow them to slip out.

She realized then how similar she and this woman were, held back by their titles.

The woman is a sorceress and a Queen.

"Set them free," Valerie said, and the guard swivelled around. "But your Majesty, they have committed theft-"

"I have made my order clear," Valerie replied coldly, and the guard bowed, then turned towards the cell, her hand reaching for the key on her belt. The sound of the cell door clanging open was accompanied by the voices of other prisoners from further in the dungeon, some laughing, some crying. The guards stationed between each of the cells did not flinch as the sorcerer stepped out of the cell, her babe pressed to her chest. A look of thankfulness crossed her face as she beheld the queen.

"Thank you, Your Majesty," she said, and Valerie smiled softly. The woman bowed quickly. But before the guard could escort her, Valerie leaned into the guard's ear.

"Have two loaves of bread given to her before she leaves." The guard didn't say anything but nodded before escorting the woman out of the dungeon.

The sound of screaming followed her on her way out.

The king and queen joined Valerie in the dining hall shortly after the sun had set. The smell of rot hadn't left her nose. The king and queen sat opposite each other on the long table, with Valerie at the head of the table. The servants wasted no time in bringing out the various courses.

As the smell of food wafted into the room, Valerie couldn't stop her mind from drifting to the sorcerer woman's face when she had told the guard to give her bread. It was a sense of thankfulness that bloomed from having something you shouldn't lack.

Were people starving in Linra? Were people dying inside her borders?

"Are you enjoying the food?" Valerie asked politely after a few minutes, her free hand clutched her skirt as she watched the king and queen. The queen nodded with a smile gracing her lips, and she sipped her water before answering.

"It's divine," she said, and Valerie knew that even if the food tasted like cow waste, she would still say it tasted heavenly. The queen's hand continuously drifted down to her stomach, and Valerie observed her for a few more seconds before she cleared her throat softly.

"How far along are you?" she asked in her soft voice. The moonlight had begun to slowly filter in through the windows that lined the circular room, and the guards stationed around the room didn't move as Valerie prompted the queen.

"Only a few weeks," the queen replied with the happiness of a proud new mother.

Her hand rested on her stomach again, and she cast her husband a joyful glance.

Most children born to royalty were born only because an heir was needed. The joy in the queen's eyes made it evident that the baby was very much wanted, not just for the crown.

"Congratulations," Valerie said, genuinely meaning it. She didn't know if she would ever have children. Her advisors had informed her of Prince Castiler's desire to court her. Her jaw clenched slightly as she thought of marriage. Had the court advisors proposed the union while her mother was still alive, she would have rebuked them for even suggesting she was wed. Her mother had always believed she didn't need a man to be a good queen. But her advisors had different ideas.

She had the right to deny a king the kingdom, and yet that would mean that if she died, her kingdom would have no successor. The room fell silent as she remembered this proposition. After a while, the king and queen excused themselves to their room, leaving Valerie to sit there for a moment, her hands shaking, where they clenched in her dress.

She didn't remember returning to her room, only that when she did, she collapsed onto her bed, not even bothering to get undressed.

Chapter 7

Valerie awoke gasping, sitting upright in bed as she gripped her chest. She could still feel the water climbing its way up her body like a serpent. Her hands shook slightly as she rubbed her face, relief flooding her that the dream was over. The sun was creeping towards the horizon, faint traces of pink and orange visible on the edge of the water. Her hands shook as she slowly pushed herself off the bed. Her head throbbed, and she found herself walking towards the balcony before she could stop herself. The glass-panelled doors opened, revealing a circular balcony with a marble railing meticulously carved.

The ocean stretched far, boats from the harbours visible in the water. The markets in Linra were known for their fishermen and traders. Her hands stopped shaking slightly when she touched the marble balcony, the ocean breeze whipping through her dishevelled curls. Gulls cried above, and below, she could see the town opening onto the docks and then the water.

She squeezed her eyes shut, absorbing the sensation of the breeze on her neck and the saltiness of the ocean, far from her reach. Her mind always felt most at peace in the presence of the sea.

Her nightmares hadn't been kind as of late. All the death surrounding her, accompanied by her weight to rule, had compressed her dreams into cruel things. Valerie could still feel the fur of the black cat curling around her ankle, the water covering her whole body, before she gasped awake.

But the voice.

That voice still filled her mind in echoes.

No need to be afraid, dear. Wake.

She knew it was all a figment of her imagination. Yet something unsettled her deeply. She was a queen; she could show no fear to the outside world. It was a weakness. She would not be weak.

She often forgot she was eighteen years old, who had been put on a throne to rule a nation on the brink of invasion or war.

Her thoughts were interrupted by the sound of the servant scuffling into her room, the woman with the patches of white skin.

"Good morning, Your Majesty," she said, dropping into a bow at the doors leading towards the balcony. Valerie felt her head fall forward in exhaustion.

"Is something wrong, my Lady?"

"No, nothing that concerns you. A nightmare is all," Valerie responded, and the servant girl nodded as if she understood.

"My mother always said a day in the sunlight would ease nightmares." The words pulled Valerie out of her thoughts, and she turned and met the servant's eyes. She didn't say anything, but there was a quiet understanding between the two of them. The girl blinked as if she remembered why she had come to her room in the first place.

"Shall I draw you a bath?" She asked, her voice quiet. Valerie could still remember the water that had crawled up her body, drowning her.

"No."

The servant nodded and made her way towards the closet to find something for Valerie to wear. Callus had sent a new decree for her to read over that morning before they met the next day. She lost a quiet breath. Valerie had never thought she would have to rule alone; she had always assumed her mother and father would guide her. And yet she was left to rule by her conscience.

Her mind was still spinning from the dream.

She felt as if the cat's tail was still curled around her ankle.

Valerie made it her mission to see the ocean. She had convinced herself that the servant girl's advice might help ease her conscience. The blue waters always had a way of bringing peace.

By the time she made her way down to the small town, everyone had awoken. Street vendors calling out their wares, children chasing each other through the streets, and women chattering at street corners. Valerie wore a white sundress that dipped low on her chest, skirt flowing around her ankles. Seraphina had insisted she accompany Valerie to the beach, but Valerie had insisted on attending alone.

If she could not go to her people unaccompanied, she would appear afraid. Fear made nobles fall. The white pillars of townhouses greeted her, and children marvelled as they saw her walking past. She found herself watching them with a softness she hadn't felt before.

The sound of the waves crashing against the shore drew her attention away from the people, and her gaze lingered on the blue waters that slowly neared. Her entire body felt drawn to the ocean, even though her dream had been nothing short of horrific. Valerie forced herself to forget the dream, but that voice was still echoing in her head.

The cobblestone pathway ended, branching onto a small wooden dock that led to the water. On either side of the small strip of beach, there were ships lined up to start docking, and sailors and fishermen were busy loading and unloading cargo from the vessels.

As she neared the water, that fear crept up into the pit of her stomach, her heartbeat thundered in her ears as she remembered the feeling of drowning. Valerie spotted the hills on the side of the small harbour.

Without hesitation, Valerie made her way across the beach, her boots in her hand as her feet dug into the soft sand. The wind whipped past her as she reached the end of the strip, past the docking ships. The caves were secluded, used only once or twice every year to watch the rise and fall of the full moon. Her eyes turned to the sky, where gulls screeched, circling the water.

The clouds were slowly gathering on the horizon. If they were lucky, Linra would experience rain that night.

After a few minutes of quiet observation, Valerie neared the stone steps carved from the cave wall. She climbed them, holding onto the wall for purchase. Her bare feet dug into the wet stone as she climbed her way up. The caves cut into the side of the dome were rumoured to have been created by the gods themselves.

Her hands scraped against the stone as she climbed past the first cave, higher. She gazed down the narrow path and saw the waves crashing against the shore, with people scattered on the beach, basking in the sun. Ships had begun to move out to sea, returning with shipments from Lunivere or Dramira, if they were lucky.

Finally, Valerie found a small cave far from the people. She stopped and peeked inside. It was dark, but sunlight was slowly filtering into the space. Ducking under the entrance, she found a small patch of stone and sat down. Her legs folded neatly under her, and she had just enough space to gaze out at the ocean below.

For the first time in days, Valerie felt like she could finally breathe. She let out a sigh, dropping her boots beside her and taking a moment to close her eyes, feeling the warmth of the sun against her freckled skin.

High above in the cave, no water would be able to reach her. And in that moment, her nightmare seemed utterly silly, nothing more than a childish fear. The gulls screeched high above the harbour, calling to one another in a way only they could understand. She hummed quietly to herself as she drew her fingers through a bit of sand on the ground beside her.

And for but a moment, all the worries, the nightmare, and that little voice inside her head went still, and she was just a girl in love with the idea of freedom.

Chapter 8

Darkness.

That's how the dreams started. Valerie stood in a room of complete and utter darkness, her hands trying to grasp something, anything to hold onto, but found nothing. She spun around in one spot, not sure where she was.

Her feet seemed to be in a pool of sorts, and as she reached down with her hand, the tips of her fingers came back wet. Across the surface of the water, a single shape walked. At first, it seemed to be a large mouse, but upon closer examination, Valerie saw that it had taken the form of a cat.

It skulked across the water as if it had been made to walk across the water unhindered. Its black fur blended into the surroundings as it slowly crept closer, and Valerie took a step back. She tried to pinch herself to wake up, but it was no use.

Strange.

The cat's pine green eyes fixated on her, much like a human would. Valerie stopped moving entirely, her feet planted in the shallow water as the cat slowly crept closer. It reached her foot and, as a cat would, it rubbed itself against her leg, tail curling around her calf for an instant before it slipped away. The caress of a lover. She tried to blink and wake up, but no matter how hard she pinched herself, the dream wouldn't stop. Just as fear seized her chest, a voice purred into the space.

No need to be afraid, dear.

The voice echoed, and as Valerie spun, she could find no face, no figure to see who it was. She knew it was only a dream, and yet she did not dare ask who it was.

Her mind fogged, and suddenly she realized that the water at her feet had begun to creep slowly up her leg - she was sinking. She didn't try to claw her way out; she kicked her legs to get back to the surface.

Just as the water hit her nose, the voice whispered one more word.

Wake.

Chapter 9

It was the day of her nineteenth birthday. The palace was in chaos.

Servants were running up and down the stairs to set up the throne room for that evening. Valerie had been so preoccupied with planning everything that the day before had passed in a blur of colours, tastings, and chatter.

Her mind was still lingering on her dream, but the constant demand to make everything perfect kept her mind at ease. Jezebel had spent nearly three hours the previous day finishing the dress, and Valerie could tell by the tired look in her eyes that the woman had worked on the dress overnight.

Jezebel fashioned the beautiful dress around her body for the final look, jewelry already set out, servants ready to do her hair. Guests would be arriving within the hour, and the throne room was fully prepared to accept the onslaught of guests. The palace chefs were done cooking the meals, and the royal musicians were at their ready. The tables were moved closer to the walls of the throne room to create space for dancing. Since her birth was nothing of absolute significance, the King and Queen of Dramira and Lunivere alike did not plan to attend that gala that evening. A part of her chest stung at that.

Guards were posted at every corner of the room and at the palace entrance. Of course, it was a masquerade party. The servants had insisted that a masquerade ball was the only proper way to celebrate something as significant as the Queen's birthday. Her mask sat untouched on the dresser, matching the dark blue of her dress and adding a mysterious quality to her appearance.

At the gala, she could be one of the people, no crown, only a mask that could hide her face from view. It was perfect.

By the time Jezebel had finished the dress, the guests were starting to arrive. From her bedroom window, the palace gardens were visible, and the steady flow of people was trickling into the throne room.

The servants had insisted she make a grand entrance from the top of the stairwell into the throne room. She hated the idea, but would do it nonetheless.

Her hair was left to fall in tight curls down her back, black shoes hidden under the dress's billowing figure. The dress itself was nothing short of a dream. The blue silk cut down her chest, revealing generous cleavage; sleeves reached her wrists and flared slightly to avoid being too tight. The waist was cinched by a corset intricately tied in the back, finished with a dark blue ribbon. She dared a glance in the mirror and found her breath swept away; it was beautiful.

Jezebel stood to the side, admiring her work from a short distance, her eyes alight with a sense of wonder. Valerie stepped off the small wooden block, her eyes unable to leave the dress. She opened her mouth to thank Jezebel for all her hard work, but a servant stormed into the room.

"The guests are all here, Your Majesty." Valerie nodded to the servant and plucked her mask from the dresser. With a nod of thanks to Jezebel, she followed the servant. The mask was fashioned with a black bow that would be tied behind her head; its shape would cover the top of her face, leaving only her eyes exposed.

The servant led her towards the stairwell, her feet moving swiftly. They reached the top of the swooping stairwell, and Valerie took a moment to hold her breath. She felt dread clawing at her gut as the servant bowed and stepped to the side. Down below, she could hear all the chattering of the people, all the whispers and murmurs as to where she was. Without further delay, she lifted her skirt and started on her way down the stairs.

The structure curved towards the end, which kept her hidden for a few steps, but upon entering the light, everyone went silent. Grays, blues, and silver scattered the ballroom. Not many were dressed in extravagant gowns and suits. Her hands resisted the urge to clutch her gown as she slowly made her way down the center stairwell. Every face in the room wore a mask that complemented their attire.

Her palms started to sweat, and she resisted the nagging feeling to rub them off on the blue silk. She reached the bottom, and people began bowing low. Her servants had not told her to make a speech, and yet the quietness was almost unsettling. After a few moments, the ballroom all rose to their full height. She made her way through the crowd, accepting congratulations and wishes, so much for keeping a secret.

The royal musicians played the first song. She did not recognize it at first, but the swooping sound of violins and the cello filled the room. People broke off to speak to each other. Some of her advisors were spotted around the room, Callus with his wife chattering about something she couldn't pick up on. Arminia stationed her guards' uniforms along the side of the room, discussing escape routes with Seraphina. Her friend glanced over for a moment and nodded, a small smile tugging at her usually set mouth.

The chandelier high above them shed light on the entire room, glowing softly.

The tables were set with beautiful light-blue tablecloths and pearl-like centrepieces. Plates were put on each table, with no names to mark each spot.

Her eighteenth birthday had been much like this one.

The same look at the throne room, the only difference was that there were no masks, and of course, her mother had planned the entire thing as a strategy to win the people's favour for her.

Valerie felt her eyes flutter close at the memory; the thought distracted her, and a moment later, she slammed into someone. Her eyes snapped open, and she tried to steady herself by grabbing onto the wall nearby, but a hand reached her forearm first, tugging her upright.

"My apologies, Your Majesty," the voice was sure and apologetic. Valerie looked up and froze for a moment. The man standing before her was nothing short of mesmerizing. The suit he wore was tailored perfectly to his broad build, and the mask was that of a bird, revealing eyes that, for a moment, left her speechless.

They were the colour of fresh honey, with flecks of a dark brown that brought out the black pupil. His skin was a tan white, with small scars and blemishes, but it made him look like a painting. His white hair was an unruly mess atop his head, falling in wisps past his mask, and for a moment, she was struck speechless.

The man's lips quivered into a smirk at her examination as if finding something amusing.

"It's alright, I shouldn't keep my eyes closed while wandering," Valerie said and slowly pulled her hand out of his grip. The man, unlike everyone else in the room, did not bow to her once more; instead, he tipped his head in a slight nod of recognition.

"I know it must seem abrupt of me, but may I have the honour of the first dance?"

For a moment, she was stunned; no one had asked her for the first dance, but she forced herself to be polite.

"Of course," she said, her hands folding neatly in front of her body. "May I ask your name?"

The man did not answer; instead, he smiled almost mischievously.

"I would rather we remain unacquainted for the time being." He said and disappeared into the crowd without a second glance. Valerie stood there stunned, her heart pounding in her chest.

Her hands interlaced, and for a moment she stood there silently before making her way through the crowd once more. Traitorously, her eyes continued to search for the head of white hair in the crowd, but could not find him.

By the time the first dance was to take place, the hours had bled past. A hundred congratulations had been said to Valerie, and a hundred times over, she had thanked the guests and smiled gratefully.

The man had not congratulated her, and that stuck in the back of her head.

The whispers started before the first dance: who would dance with the queen first, who had dared to ask her for a dance. Other than the man, no one else had asked her, and that sent a sting through her chest. At least five dances were awaiting her, and she knew she would only dance one.

By the time the first dance was about to commence, no one else had asked her. Her mind was spinning before that voice appeared close to her ear.

"Miss me already?"

There was something boyish about his voice that seemed to catch her off guard. Upon turning, she saw him standing there, his gloved hand outstretched while the other was folded behind his back. Just as the ballad started, she found herself taking his hand. Her palm fit in his almost perfectly, and she tried to stop the flutter in her stomach. She was to marry the prince of Dramira; she could not allow herself to be flattered by just anyone. Without a moment to waste, he led her onto the now clear floor, and a few of the other couples led their partners onto the small space.

"Missing you would imply I know you," she said after a while, her voice sounding almost uncertain. He let out a small chuckle.

"You are rather intelligent," he said, and she feigned a look of shock.

"Are you implying all queens are stupid?" she said as he finally stood before her fully. His one hand dropped to her waist while the other took her hand in his. Automatically, her other hand rested on his firm shoulder. Those golden eyes met hers once more as they began to move with the music.

"No, I would never make such an accusation; it might cost me my head," he said, and she could tell he was being sarcastic. He twirled her once and pulled her back to his chest. She noticed how all the eyes in the ballroom had flitted at her.

"You do seem like the sort of gentleman who values his head," she said, which earned another soft laugh that sent heat flaring in her chest. Traitor.

"Might I ask you for your name now, since we have shared almost a full dance?" She said, and his eyes were slightly harder as he turned back to her, leading her away from his body.

"It is only fair if I know yours first," he said with a soft sort of tone as if he were afraid to startle her.

Did he honestly not know who she was? As if he knew what she was thinking, he leaned a bit closer.

"I know who you are, but I would much rather hear your name from your lips than others." He said, and she felt a flush creep up her neck. He had a way of speaking that caught her off guard.

"Valerie," she said hesitantly, and he smiled softly, revealing a dimple at the edge of his mask.

"Valerie," he repeated, and when he said it, she realized how it might seem beautiful to others; it was the name her father had chosen. The first song ended abruptly, and for a moment, the couples scattered to find new suitors to dance with. The man in front of her had not departed from her; he watched her curiously.

"No other courtiers asked for a dance?"

She felt a flush creep up her neck again as she shook her head slightly.

"No."

He let out a laugh, and she got the impression he was mocking her. She would not be mocked at her gala. She pulled her hand out of his grasp, but he caught her wrist.

"I am not mocking you. I am merely laughing at the other courtiers' stupidity." She stood there stunned, her heart beating loudly in her ears.

"Since there are no others who might ask for a dance, might I ask for the next?"

She found her breath momentarily stolen, and she swallowed. He was being relatively straightforward. She knew she should say no, decline the choice of dancing with him, but…

"If you intend to live up to your previous skills in dance, then yes," she said. Her voice became more confident as she stepped back into his arms, her hand settling on his shoulder while the other lay nestled in the crease of his palm.

"If you insist, Your Majesty," he purred, and in that moment, she forgot the ballroom, the weight of the court, everything. And lost herself in a pair of golden eyes, as he led her into another dance.

"You never told me your name," she said as he spun her again.

His face was inches from hers when he whispered it, quietly enough that she almost missed it.

"You can call me Emris."

Chapter 10

His name sent a shiver down her spine. She met his eyes, and after a moment, her curiosity got hold of her.

"You're not from Cyneria. Are you?" She said more of a statement than a question, and his smirk seemed to vanish for a moment.

"What makes you think that?" he said, dipping her low as the violins continued their ballad. The hair at the back of her neck seemed to stand up, and she became aware of every guard in the room. For a moment, she felt dread deep in her gut.

"You seem frightened," he said, his breath tickling her ear, her hand tensed on his shoulder, and she started to look for a guard who would pay attention.

"I don't get scared easily," she said, and his eyes raked over her body quickly.

"Lying isn't your specialty, Your Majesty," he said, and his voice dropped to the point where she felt fear tighten in her gut, ears throbbing with her heartbeat. In that moment, the same feeling from her nightmares filled her mind. For a moment, she froze in his arms. It seemed like the whole room froze for a moment.

"Why are you here?" she asked, her voice trembling, and for a moment he cocked his head.

"She didn't tell you?" He asked, freezing as well; his hand didn't tighten on her waist, but for a moment, she couldn't breathe. The world stopped for a moment; her body tensed up as she racked her brain.

"Who? Seraphina?"

None of her advisors had mentioned anyone by name. For a moment, she stood there, brows furrowed underneath the mask, her eyes blank as she looked at him.

She felt real fear coursing through her veins. She tried to pull away, but his head dropped to her neck. Slightly, his breath tickled her shoulder. He leaned in to whisper.

"You don't know, do you?" He purred, and she felt herself starting to breathe heavier.

"Are you here to kill me?" She asked in her rough voice as she squeezed her eyes shut. She knew how to disarm an attacker; her mother's assassination had made her train in her minimal spare time. In the darkness of night, when she couldn't sleep.

Her eyes traced every line of his face, as if she could memorize it for a moment.

His hand tightened on hers,

"No," he breathed out, almost disappointed. She was aware that assassins had tried to kill her alongside her mother all those months ago; he could be another one sent to murder her in cold blood at her gala.

"So, you have no idea," he said, almost miserably, his face contorted into shock, and she shook her head. His head dropped low again, and they stopped dancing as the second ballad made its final crescendo to an ending.

"I would rather we speak in private," he said, and she felt her jaw clench. He could take her somewhere to kill her, or he could be using this as an opportunity to get her away from her guards.

"I would rather not…"

"You misunderstand me; it wasn't a request."

Her gut clenched, and she felt her entire body lock up. He was threatening her, and she forced her eyes to remain on his face even as her breath hitched. Without another word, she started to walk, her arm hooked into the crook of his elbow, and she made her way to the balcony doors, trying to catch hold of Seraphina's eyes but failing to find her friend in the crowd. Her pulse raced as they finally reached the doors; he opened them, and the cool air hit her hot skin.

The doors closed behind them, and for a moment she stood there, her arm hooked in his. She took a moment to appear calm before she slipped her hand out of his grasp so she could face him. The ocean crashed in the distance, and for a moment, she met his eyes again. The stars shone down on them.

"You dare threaten a queen in her palace," she snapped, her anger flaring hot in her stomach. She was usually good at containing her temper, but now she felt nothing but rage.

He chuckled darkly, and she felt herself backing up slightly to get a grip on the stone railing. He took a careful step closer, his hands shoving into his pockets. He examined her for a moment before he let out a breath.

"I suppose you deserve an explanation."

"I suppose I do," she responded, anger still dripping from her voice.

Emris took a step back to lean against the raised. He examined her for another moment, taking in every detail of her mask, her dress, her mouth, and her hands clenched tightly.

"You've heard her voice, I'm assuming," he said, his arms crossed.

"I do not know who you are referring to," she snapped. "If you are referring to General Arminia, then yes," she said, and he chuckled again.

"Do not laugh at me," she spat, her hands clenching tighter, nails digging into her palm. His eyes turned serious as he watched her; his eyes seemed to glow in the darkness, like a snake ready to strike.

"I am starting to think you have no idea what you have become."

At the words, she felt her chest filled with dread. What could he mean? She was the Queen, the last remaining blood relative to the Denisera name. What else could she possibly be? He took a step closer, and she backed up into the railing. The wind whipped around them, and for a moment, the idea of her falling filled her mind.

"And what is that?" She asked, fear slipping into her voice, and he took another step forward. He did not answer her, but as if in response, a voice filled her head, sending her knees buckling.

Mine.

It was the voice of the woman from her dreams, and it echoed in her head for a moment, and her eyes widened. Shivers shot throughout her entire body as she swallowed. Valerie closed her eyes; she tried to convince herself that it was an illusion. Her mouth fell open slightly, and nausea coursed to the surface of her throat.

"She's in there, isn't she?" He asked, stepping closer, and her hand shot out to stop him, but he continued his slow approach.

"Stop," she begged. She didn't know if she was speaking to the voice in her head or him. But in that moment, fear drowned her like the waves in her dream.

"You cannot escape her, Valerie," he said, and she found herself growing tired of his games. She squeezed her eyes shut once more, and when she opened them, his hand was around the back of her head. In a moment, the mask fell away, and her face was bared to him. He took a long moment to observe her before his hand came up to cradle her jaw.

"Look at me."

He snarled, and for a moment, she found anger so deep in her guts that when she opened her eyes, rage flared in those brown eyes. So deep that for a moment he seemed entranced.

His hand was still on her jaw, and for a moment, she felt fear mixed with rage. Without knowing what she was doing, she pushed him hard, and he stumbled back. And for a moment, he stood there stunned, but he did not approach her again.

"She really is in there," he whispered, almost in recognition of what he had just done.

"Who?" She demanded, her face burning from where he had gripped it. "Morana."

At the name, it seemed as though the stars themselves disappeared out of the sky, and the voice that slithered out of her mouth wasn't her own.

"Hello, Emris."

Chapter 11

Emris had never heard the voice that came from Valerie's mouth.

But from the moment he did, terror seized him. He had faced gods before, but never Morana. Valerie did not know what she possessed.

Valerie looked at him with a rage that he had seen in many before her. Confusion raised her brow. But that voice.

Valerie closed her mouth as if she couldn't understand what she had done. Ciro had warned him to be careful, his voice throbbing in the back of his head as he beheld the shadows that curled around Valerie. She did not seem to notice them, yet her brown eyes glowed with a darker power.

"Holy gods," he choked out, and she stood there. Before he could say anything more, he felt Ciro's presence.

I can't hold her back.

Ciro's deep voice whispered in the back of his head, and he barely had time to steel himself before a sharp pain flashed through his head. The barrier around his mind collapsed as another voice slid into his head.

Following me, Emris?

Morana purred. Valerie stood there shaking slightly. The shadows had receded, and his head pounded as he beheld her. Morana gave another sharp tug on his mind, pain flaring in his temple as he grunted.

I would rather you answer me before I choke Ciro out of you.

The threat was icy, but Morana did not make threats she wasn't intending to keep.

Hello Morana.

Ciro answered deep inside his head, both of the gods speaking to each other as if they hadn't for decades. Emris knew they hadn't.

How long have you been following me? Morana purred, and Emris felt his temple flare; his hands itched to rip the mask from his face.

How long have you been inhabiting Valerie? Ciro asked. Morana let out a dark chuckle.

Fool. She replied, and Emris gasped slightly as Morana's presence left his head. Valerie was still shaking by the time the shadows receded from around her body. Emris watched as her eyes filled with fear.

"What was that?"

Valerie's voice cut through the air like a knife, and it took Emris a few moments of breathing deeply before he took a step closer. He was careful not to get too close, as Morana seemed annoyed enough. One wrong move and she would strangle Ciro out of him.

"That was Morana."

"What is she doing inside my head?" She asked, her voice shaking terribly as she clutched her skirt like it could anchor her to the ground. Emris' head still throbbed from Morana's presence. His hands were shaking slightly. Morana was robust, powerful enough that even Ciro was silent in his head. Ciro was never quiet.

"I can't breathe," she gasped, clutching her chest, and before Emris could try to calm her down, her eyes fluttered shut, and she tilted. He was moving before he knew what he was doing. If Valerie got hurt, Morana would flare, and she would kill him, most likely. He caught her before she hit the ground. She was unconscious, having no doubt fainted from the shock.

He put one hand under her knees, the dress folding over his arm, the other behind her back, her head against his chest. Her curls fell past his arm, and he looked at her for a moment. Morana didn't reach out again; she was silent. And that scared him more than it eased him.

He made his way back to the balcony door, but before he could even reach for the handle, it swung open. A guard dressed in silver armour stepped outside the door, opening it behind her, black cropped hair swaying as her eyes flicked to Valerie in his arms.

"What happened?" The woman demanded, her hand on the hilt of her sword as she stepped fully outside.

"She had fainted. We were talking, and she just..."

The woman looked down at Valerie.

"We need to get her to the healer," the woman said and opened the door, her silver armour catching the light. Emris knew the word 'we' meant that he was going to carry her. Valerie lay limp in his arms as he followed the guard. She led the two of them around the fray of people to another stairwell on the furthest side of the ballroom, concealed enough that none of the guests noticed the queen in his arms. She stirred faintly against his chest, but he didn't glance down.

The guard led him up the flight of stairs, down a series of hallways, before arriving at a set of double doors. With a swift hand, she opened them. Emris followed her into what was no doubt Valerie's room. He took a moment to take in the large bed, the plush carpet on the stone floor. The balcony door was closed, and moonlight filtered into the room through a few windows.

The woman gestured for Emris to put her down on the bed. He took a few steps toward the white mattress and slowly slid her down onto it. Her weight, leaving his arms, was almost unnoticeable. He had carried grown men out of harm's way; she weighed little to nothing for him.

The guard called for a servant down the hall, and when the small woman rushed into the room, the guard instructed her to get the healer. Only when the servant disappeared did Emris turn to the guard. She turned back to him, hand still on the hilt of her sword as if hesitant about his real reason for being outside with Valerie.

"Thank you for taking care of her," the guard said, and after a moment, she took a step closer to the bed. He did not remember what else the guard said, for Morana's voice filled his head once more.

Leave.

The hair on the back of his neck stood up, but he mustered the willpower to respond in his head to the goddess's voice.

If she does not survive, you will have no one to inhabit.

With that, he made his way to the seat opposite the bed. The guard did not question his motive; she was busy, speaking with the healer about what had happened. Only then did he reach back and untie the mask from around his face. He swore that Morana laughed inside his head.

Chapter 12

Valerie woke with her head throbbing. No nightmares had followed her into unconsciousness, but the reminder of Morana's voice in her head, speaking through her mouth to Emris.

Her mind blanked as she turned her head, eyes scanning the room. Someone had changed her out of her dress into a white chemise, her hair was messy against the pillow, and her neck ached as she sat up on her elbows.

"You've been out for hours."

Emris's voice cut through the air like a blade. She turned and saw him sitting in the chair beside the bed, elbows on his knees, hunched forward. Seeing him made all those memories flash through her mind. She pushed him back, and he grunted in pain, doubling over, before she collapsed from shock. She still couldn't explain the voice inside her head, and a shiver coursed through her.

Her eyes latched onto Emris and refused to blink. She should call Seraphina and tell her to send him to the dungeon. He had laid his hands on her. Her fists clenched the blanket. Her gaze narrowed on him, and she sat up straighter. He had removed his mask; he was even more devastatingly handsome without it.

As much as she wanted to call for Seraphina, she knew he was the only one who had any understanding about what Morana was doing inside her head. He knew more than she; if he could give her an answer, then she would keep him around.

"What are you doing here?" She demanded as loudly as she could, her voice hoarse. He sat up straighter, holding his mask in his hands. After a moment, he put it down on the floor.

His golden eyes latched onto hers, his high cheekbones, and a fine mouth no longer obscured by the mask. His suit was slightly rumpled and slightly unbuttoned.

Her mind was spinning.

She had remembered looking at him, unable to breathe, and then darkness surrounding her.

How had she gotten back to her room?

"It seems you still want answers," he said, looking up. She had a dagger in the cabinet beside her bed; if she moved fast enough, she could get her hands on it. She wouldn't be able to kill him, but she could hurt him, no doubt.

How had Seraphina let him stay?

She did not know, but one thing was sure: he needed answers as badly as she did.

Because if whatever he had said so far was true -

She couldn't think about it. She pressed a palm to her eye, head still throbbing. If he wanted to fool her, fine, but she needed him for answers.

"It seems you need answers too," she quipped, wincing as she forced her legs to shift under the blankets. A servant entered the room just as Emris opened his mouth. The servant bowed upon reaching the foot of the bed. Emris did not speak as the servant stood.

"All the guests have left the palace, and General Seraphina has told me she will come to see you shortly."

"Thank you," Valerie said with a nod of her head. "Do you need anything, Milady?"

Valerie opened her mouth to ask for another guard-

"Water," Emris said, and the servant looked at him. He feigned a polite smile, and the servant gave an annoyed glance but nodded nonetheless, disappearing from the room. Valerie glared at him.

"I've been sitting here for hours; the least I could have is a glass of water," Emris told Valerie, like she cared whether he lived or died. If anything, he could be tricking her into some scheme to kill her. She had to admit it was unlikely since she was still alive. Her fingers itched to reach for her dagger.

She scoffed and swung her legs off the bed, watching him the whole time. His eyes tracked her like a predator as she slowly walked towards the door, opened it, and found that no guards were stationed outside. As much as she dreaded being alone with Emris, someone who no doubt wanted more from her than he had let on, she needed to understand what the hell had happened on that balcony. And if the voice was still inside her head.

She sighed, turning back to him; his eyes had not left her.

"What do you want?" She asked, slowly moving towards him, her bare feet padding softly on the ground, her hand clenched in her skirt.

"Come again?" He asked almost coyly. "What is it you want? Silver?"

He laughed, and she found that rage coiled in her gut again.

"If I wanted silver, trust me, I would not have come to you." He waited, bit his lip, and stood. He walked closer, her hands clenched tightly in anger.

Gods, she had been infatuated with him earlier that night.

"I know what you are. And I know who is in your head," he whispered almost understandingly. She wanted to say he didn't, that he had no idea what he was talking about. But the way his eyes had widened upon hearing that woman's voice out of her mouth made it clear he knew more about her than she knew about herself.

And that scared her.

"Your mother hated sorcerers; she murdered thousands of them in cold blood. And now you," he said, taking a step closer as if building suspense, "are the new queen." He laughed again, and she found her jaw clenching.

"What?!" She spat, and his eyes snapped towards her. "No, I just find it terribly ironic."

"What?!"

He took another step; he was close enough that she could smell the jasmine and honey on his skin. Close enough that a shiver traced up her spine. She watched him closely, eyes never leaving his as he leaned in closely.

"Because the daughter of the murderer of thousands of sorcerers, the newly crowned queen of Cyneria, is a conduit."

She barely had a moment to understand before a knock sounded at the door.

The servant beheld them standing inches apart and bowed in apology. His eyes didn't leave Valerie as he took the glass from the servant's hand. Valerie felt her face pale at his words. The servant most likely hadn't heard his words. She looked at the two of them and silently left the room.

For a moment, she just stood there, hands now slack at her sides. It was impossible. She couldn't be a conduit. Humans were rarely selected as conduits, and even if they were, they were usually born conduits. She had been human all her life. She stumbled backwards; her voice stuck in her throat. She watched him with eyes now full of fear. Not of him, but the words that he had spoken, of the uprooting it could bring.

"You're lying," she whispered, and he moved towards her dresser, placing the now-empty glass down on the bedside. He turned back to her, undoing the button of his cravat, as he slowly walked towards her again.

"Maybe, but we both know that the voice inside your head is not of yourself." He said, and she swallowed. He sat down on the chair once more and observed her as she made her way to the wall, gripping it tightly for balance.

If what he said were true, she would be dethroned and executed. Her mother had killed thousands of sorcerers and magic wielders simply because they were creations of the gods. What would they do to her if she were a conduit - a living extension of a god?

Her hands shook, and her eyes squeezed shut.

"Do you seriously believe that I would lie to you about something so serious?" He asked, and in that moment her rage took over again.

"Shut up," she snarled. Her mind was everywhere and nowhere at once. When she looked back over at him, she saw the smile tugging at his mouth, and tears of anger filled her throat.

He sat back, not speaking as she watched him.

"How do you know all this?" She demanded, her hands still shaking.

"That would be a longer conversation," he said, "and if I am not mistaken, as soon as your guard comes to check on you, you will have me executed." He said this as if this were a casual conversation, running a hand through his hair, watching her intently.

She wished she could say he was lying, yet the possibility played around in her head. If he were lying just to get closer to her and kill her, then she would suffer, but if she got rid of him, he wouldn't be able to tell her what the hell was wrong with her.

"Tell me how you know so much about me, and I might let you live," she threatened. Whether he believed she was telling the truth or not, he straightened.

"What's it to me?"

"You'll get to speak to *her*."

At the mention, he stilled, his brow furrowing, and he looked from her eyes to her lips. Moments later, Seraphina barged in, her hand on the hilt of her sword. She stopped when she saw Valerie standing.

"Are you alright? How are you feeling?"

"I'm fine," she said softly, and Seraphina came closer to examine her as if a wound would be seen. Then her eyes flicked to Emris, and Seraphina followed her gaze.

"Do you know him?" Seraphina asked, suddenly on high alert. Seraphina must have assumed he had known her because he must have carried her back into the palace. Valerie looked at Emris, who was watching her in a cat-like manner. A shiver raced down her spine.

"Yes, I know him," she lied. It tasted sour on her tongue. Valerie had never lied to anyone before, least of all Seraphina, her dearest friend. At the words, Seraphina relaxed her hand, dropping away from her sword.

"Would you like a room prepared? Or will he not be staying long?" Seraphina asked, her eyes flicking back to Emris. If she intended to get answers, he would need to stay.

"Have a room prepared." With that, Seraphina nodded and bowed low before exiting the room. Valerie was pacing when the door shut. Emris opened his mouth to say something, but she interjected, pointing an accusatory finger directly at him.

"Do not think for one moment you are not on thin ice? The only reason you are staying is so that you can explain all of this," she gestured to herself.

Emris stood.

"While I am here, what will you tell people I am? Your friend? Your acquaintance?" She knew where he was getting at. If a mysterious man just suddenly started living in the palace, questions would undoubtedly be asked. It wasn't uncommon for queens to take lovers before they were married, and of course, the prince of Dramira had not formally courted her. Valerie's cheeks flushed as she fidgeted with her chemise.

"While you are here, which will not be long, we will pretend to be lovers." For a moment, she sounded almost shy. She had never had a lover, and the idea sent her mind fogging and her heart beating too fast. He let out a soft laugh as if he found her genuinely amusing.

"If you insist," he said, undoing the rest of his cravat. The over-shirt fell away, and he draped it over his arm. The white button down underneath did little to hide his figure. The stiff muscles sculpted on his chest were clearly visible under the fabric, and her face went red.

"And as soon as I no longer want you, you will be gone."

To this, he smirked, running a hand through his hair again.

"You have a habit of smiling, is something exceedingly amusing?"

"Do I not have the right to smile at my lover?" He purred. Her hands were suddenly sweaty, her heart thundering under her ribs, beating to get out.

"And how will you say we met?" He asked, picking at his fingernails for a moment as she stood shocked and flushed from his previous statement. She forced the unfamiliar feelings down into her gut. Forcing herself to focus on the words he said.

"Tonight, at the ball," she said, pacing again softly, "I will say you saved me from being poisoned, and after that, I took you as my lover, should anyone ask." The words sounded so unfamiliar and strange on her tongue that she turned bright red. He smirked again, his eyes fixating on her flushed expression.

"And how well do we need to play the part?" He asked, and she shot him with a glare that cut through steel. He chuckled, putting his hands up in mock surrender. By the time a servant returned to escort him to his room, she was still flushed, her hands clenched tightly. He walked by close enough that he could bend down slightly and whisper.

"See you at breakfast."

She tried not to throw the nearest object as the door finally closed behind him.

Chapter 13

Emris was led to his room by the young girl. His cravat still hung over his arm, and he followed briskly. The moonlight shone down on the coastal town of Linra, and Emris had to admit it was beautiful.

Upon his arrival, days earlier, he had taken in the beautiful beach, the harbour, and the elaborate kingdom built on cobblestone. The servant made her way to a room at the end of the hall, opposite Valerie's room. Her hands were clasped in front of her as she opened the door. He gave her a slight nod of thanks as he stepped inside and shut the door behind him. The room was laid out beautifully; a large white bed sat on one side, and a door to the bathing room was across the space. A plush white rug sat in a circle beneath the chandelier. The two large windows let in moonlight, and white gauze was pulled slightly in front of them to shield the room from too much light.

He made his way to the plush settee in front of the bed, dropping his cravat as he undid the buttons of his white shirt. His fingers worked nimbly, and after a few seconds, the shirt opened, and he slid it off easily.

You should not have made that deal, Emris.

Ciro always had an interesting way of making himself known. Yet it never caught Emris off-guard, as he had grown used to the god's voice in the back of his head and the tingling sensation that filled him upon hearing it.

What did you expect me to do?

Ciro did not respond to the statement. Emris threw his white button down on the settee and moved to undo the laces of his brown boots. Once free, he put them down neatly by the foot of the bed. He could not sleep. Not when the memory of Morana's voice sent fear coursing through him.

Ciro had not prepared him for what her voice did to people. Did not prepare him for the death that lurked in her voice. He sighed, rubbing his hands over his face.

It will all work out. Be patient.

If Ciro had not known Emris since he was a boy, he would have struck him down right there. The god did not respond. Ciro never had trouble dealing with his sarcasm. It drove Emris nearly mad.

But as Ciro's conduit, he was indebted to live out his will, and Ciro had told him to hunt down the next conduit for Morana. He knew very little about the goddess.

Emris sat himself down on the edge of the bed, his head dropping into his hands.

Morana had always been a goddess of anger rather than beauty. Yes, she was beautiful. She didn't kill men with it immediately; she lured them in like prey and then struck. After the second faerie war, when the gods had pulled back their powers from both humanity and faeries, she had been one of the only gods to keep her power in civilization. She hand-picked her conduits. Nearly every one of them went mad. He could not recall every conduit, but he knew there was a pattern to them.

Humans.

She had never picked a faerie to be her conduit. Some of the gods did not care who was picked; instead, they cared about what they could do. Emris couldn't wrap his head around why Morana would pick Valerie.

She was a newly orphaned daughter of two war generals. She had no power other than her kingdom, and she was newly crowned. What could that bring to Morana that she could not find in a faerie?

Naivety.

Ciro answered for him, and for a moment, it all made sense to Emris. Where faeries knew right from wrong, having lived longer than humans and could discern between their conscience and the impulse of a god, humans were like babes. They did not know what their own impulse was, and what they weren't.

Morana had driven her previous conduits mad and convinced them that it was all for their own good. No one had ever been able to tame Morana.

Where Ciro was level-headed and aimed to keep Emris alive, Morana used her conduit's body as a pawn, building them up and destroying them if it meant she got one thing.

Power.

By the time a servant came to announce breakfast was ready, he had been awake for an hour. He had been staring out the window at the ocean crashing far away. He hadn't seen the sea since he arrived a few days prior, and he missed the smell of salt and the wind ruffling his hair.

He dressed in the white button-down and boots he had worn the previous night. He knew Valerie would no doubt have clothes prepared for him if he were to play her lover for the time being.

He followed the servant girl down the stairs to the dining hall. Valerie was seated at the end of the table, wearing a light blue dress that grazed the floor, her eyes fixed on the food on her plate. The room was filled with sunlight, and a soft breeze gently flowed through it. Guards stood around the room, positioned closest to the different windows.

As soon as her chocolate brown eyes met his, they hardened.

"Good morning," he said with a slight bow before making his way to the chair on her right. Although there were many different places he could sit, if they were to pose as lovers, they'd better get off to a good start.

"Morning," she replied almost stiffly. He could tell by the tired look in her eyes that she hadn't gotten enough sleep. Ciro never kept him out of sleep, but Morana could be tormenting her at night. He did not let the sudden surge of empathy show.

"We have much to discuss today," she said, gesturing for him to eat the food. Eggs had been scrambled with a few herbs, bread cut and coated with butter, and a small glass of juice sat in front of him. He smirked, bowing his head slightly in thanks.

Her jaw clenched, and he noticed how she clutched her knife as if she were about to stab him. He had been convinced that the night before, he would have been executed, or, at the very least, imprisoned for laying a hand on her.

Emris could still see the look of resentment in her eyes from the incident. He didn't feel bad for being rough with her. If he had to be rough to bring forth Morana, then he would do it a hundred times over.

"Indeed, we do," he replied, picking up his fork to start eating. Over the past few days, he had nourished himself with bread he bought from a street vendor, the elderly lady smitten by his charm and offering him deals to pay less. The eggs were perfectly scrambled, and he tried not to groan at the taste. The bread, which had tasted so good in recent days, paled in comparison.

"After breakfast, we will have a walk in the gardens, where we can discuss more private matters," she said, trying to add a hint of flirtation but failing miserably. He took the moment to examine her. Without her mask, she was beautiful; he could not deny it.

Her dark brown eyes had speckles of lighter gradients, siren-shaped and framed perfectly by her high cheekbones. Her round ears were decorated with earrings, and beautiful curls framed her face. Her cheeks were slightly flushed, and her fine mouth was pressed together as if thinking. Freckles were scattered over her face like constellations, and for a moment, he was entranced. It wasn't genius, but he could not look away.

When she raised her head, sensing his attention, he held her gaze. She was stubborn, no doubt. She broke eye contact to look back down at her plate, then sipped at her juice before turning her gaze to the windows. He had seen the palace gardens upon entering the palace.

He had stolen the invite from another nobleman, and he had used his few remaining silvers to pay for a suit and a finely crafted mask. He smirked to himself. After a few more minutes of quiet eating, she finally finished her plate, and he was finished as well. Without any further hesitation, she turned to him again.

"Join me for a walk?" Her hands clenched in her lap, and the tension in her shoulders was palpable. He gave her a soft smile.

"I would be honoured," he said, and rose as soon as she had pushed away herself from the table; he extended his arm to her. The memories of the night before flashed in his mind, and when she hooked her arm through his, he tucked it into his ribs like a sacred treasure. Servants bustled into the room to clear the plates as they made their way to the front doors of the palace. The guards, standing at the ready, noticed their approach and opened the doors in a few swift motions.

Emris noticed how their eyes tracked him warily.

As soon as they stepped into the fresh air, it was as if someone had smeared a balm over her heart. Her arm relaxed slightly in his, her fingers tucked into the crook of his elbow, not clutching so tightly. He took a moment before they started to walk. Once they were a safe distance away from the palace, she slid her arm out of his grip.

The gardens unfolded before them like a labyrinth. Neatly trimmed bushes were arranged into different rows, each bearing flowers. As Valerie started to walk, he followed, close enough to speak but not close enough that she could strangle him. Which, by the look on her face, she seemed extremely tempted to do.

Emris knew she was not stronger than him, but if she got angry like she had last time, Morana would come out. And Emris knew she would not hesitate to put down a threat to her conduit.

They remained silent. Emris watched as her eyes traced the different bushes. His hand reached out to touch a rose petal. The feeling of the plant underneath his calloused hand was soft, and he was lost in the feeling for a moment.

"If you think I am going to talk about anything other than last night, you are mistaken," she said, her voice not as sharp as it had been at breakfast. He smirked inwardly. Valerie had a way of disarming his usually calm facade in seconds, which infuriated him.

"I would expect nothing less," he said, stepping forward so that he now treads beside her. His hands stuffed into his pockets, sleeves rolled up to his elbows, baring his scarred forearms to the morning sun. Her gaze flickered at them momentarily, but she said nothing.

"What would you like to know?" He asked, and she froze, turned to him with a look of annoyance. His eyes took a moment to trace her face once more.

"You are very willing to share things with me all of a sudden," she said, no doubt skeptical of his question. He took a cautious step closer, and he could see how she bristled. She did not doubt that anyone would touch her as he had, and he flinched slightly at her reaction.

"Valerie, look-"

"You will address me as Your Majesty when you are in my presence," she said, her voice suddenly stern. She was annoyed, her eyes were narrowed, and her brow furrowed.

He gave her a mock bow.

"Your Majesty, I am willing to share with you what you would like to know. As long as I get to speak with Morana again."

At the mention of her name, she flinched visibly. He could not erase the look of utter fear in her eyes when another voice - *her* voice - had spoken from her lips. Valerie stepped back slightly, her hands curling into the fabric of her gown. He knew that look.

Many of the conduits he had encountered feared their gods, yes, but this; Morana was a goddess of pure terror. He would not want her stuck in his head either. For a moment, they stood there, then she sighed, biting her lower lip for a moment before meeting his eyes,

"Tell me how you know who I am, or what I am rather."

He stepped closer and dropped his voice to a low whisper, so only she could hear.

He could smell the scent of vanilla on her, and for a moment, he just breathed it in.

"A few months ago, your mother was killed in an assassination attempt. She had been seeking out the Faerie Priestesses' scrolls from one of their temples. She wanted to know whether there would be another conduit in Cyneria. She tried to send spies into the lands, and they traced it back to her and killed her. The assassin that she had hired had gotten his hands on the scroll. He found me by accident, and I read the scroll."

He spoke the lie so convincingly that when her face paled, he knew she was reliving her mother's death. In truth, he had no idea what had truly happened to her mother, only that, yes, she had been assassinated a few months prior.

He stepped back; her eyes had glazed over, and he suddenly felt his eyes narrow. Her hand clasped her skirt, and her eyes stared right through his chest. Emris feared Morana would sense the lie and tell her, but by the look on her face — terror, anger, and confusion — he knew the goddess had said nothing.

And that scared him more than he would admit.

Chapter 14

Valerie didn't know how to believe him. It sounded nearly impossible coming from his lips. She stood there before him, the wind whipping through her hair, gulls crying above them, and she could not stop her hands from clutching her skirt like a lifeline.

Was it true?

Had her mother truly been seeking the next conduit? She knew not the practices of the faerie priestesses, but Emris no doubt knew more about them than he had let on. Her breath left her in a shaky gasp. Why had her mother even risked it?

"And the scroll told you-"

"That you would be the next conduit."

Her mind felt like a fog had settled over it. If the goddess in her head could hear her, she said nothing. She shook her head in disbelief.

"How could faerie priestesses know the will of the gods themselves?" she asked, her eyes burning. If her mother had gotten her hands on the scroll, would she have killed Valerie? The thought sent bile rising in her throat, and she squeezed her eyes shut.

"Many of the faerie priestesses receive visions from the gods; they intercede for the gods and document all their findings." He took a step forward.

"Did the scroll say why?"

Why her? Of all the people in Milornia, why her? She felt like she couldn't breathe, like the air was being constricted out of her body.

"No."

The words sent her stomach plummeting. She looked down at her feet, hands shaking as tears burned her throat. She forced her mind to clear. It couldn't be an accident, could it? There had to be a reason.

"Are you alright?" Emris asked, his hand moved to touch her elbow, and she flinched back. His golden eyes settled on her face. She did not believe for one second that his care was genuine. He was playing with her lover. He would do anything to talk to the woman inside her head. But why?

"No, I am not alright," she said, striding away from him. He followed her.

She didn't want to speak with him anymore; she wanted to disappear entirely. "Was it something I said?"

"The world does not revolve around you, Emris," she snapped. She had never said his name before, but she said it with so much anger that for a moment his smirk faded.

"Believe me, Your Majesty, I am well aware."

She felt tears of anger and confusion blur her vision, and she wiped furiously at her eyes. It should be impossible. Her mother had hated sorcerers or anything to do with the gods; she had bred a nation that hated any people with magic. How would they receive her, a conduit?

They wouldn't have realized.

She knew immediately that if this came out to anyone, she would be hanged on the gallows. She could not let her father's memory be tainted by her failure. She stopped walking abruptly, and Emris had to sidestep before he could slam into her back.

"I hate you," she spat, and his face did not drop; instead, his mouth crooked into a grin.

"Believe me, Sweetheart, the feeling is completely mutual." She felt the urge to slap him.

"If you had not shown up, none of this would have happened," she said, her hands waving in the air as if to gesture to everything that had possibly gone wrong. He stalked forward, his feet moving swiftly over the grass. Before coming down to breakfast, she had hidden a dagger in one of her pockets. She itched to reach for it, as he towered over her. He was mad, his golden eyes glowed, and his face was filled with silent anger.

"You assume that my appearance at the gala brought Morana on you?"

"Yes, of course it was you," she said, trying to walk away.

He grabbed her wrist, and she drew her dagger with her other hand. He did not flinch as the blade pressed against his throat. He merely cocked an eyebrow at her.

He did not move to drop her hand; the blade shook slightly in her grasp. His mouth pulled into a smirk as he leaned in a little closer.

"You will find that we bleed the same colour," he whispered, and she pulled the dagger away. She needed him more than she loathed him. He was infuriating, but he was also the only person who had answers for Morana.

"Do you tend to threaten a lot of men before noon, Your Majesty?" He asked, rubbing his throat softly with his hand. She wrenched her hand from his grip.

"I try not to," she answered. She had shoved the dagger into its hilt.

For a moment, they stood there staring at each other, and he huffed a breath.

"You need me for answers, so I suggest you listen to me when I tell you there is no way of escaping Morana," he said, stuffing his hands into his pockets, watching her with a predatory gaze. She felt her insides twist.

She had hoped there would be some way out of whatever hold Morana held on her. She swallowed. Her hands were clammy once more, and she resisted the urge to wipe her hands off on her dress.

"How do I get rid of her then?" She spoke in a lower voice than she would have liked. He did not laugh this time; a look of seriousness came over him as he paused to think for a moment.

"One does not rid oneself of Morana; one survives her. And I am the only person who knows how to survive the will of a god," he said as he reached down with one hand. He plucked a lavender from its stem, twirling it between his fingers for a moment, his eyes never leaving her.

"Why is that?" She asked, hands still clenched, eyes flickering to his hands before moving back to his eyes.

He stepped closer and offered the flower to her as if offering a gift to a child.

"Because although we bleed the same colour, my master is not as prone to wickedness as you might think."

"What do you mean?" she asked, looking at the flower he had offered her, voice shaking slightly in the wind. That's when a completely different voice filled her head, deeper than Morana's.

He is my conduit.

For a moment, she stood there stunned, then she began to shake. She could not explain to herself why Morana's voice had been in her head, but the voice inside her head was deeper, silkier, and reminded her of Emris.

"Get out of my head," she bit at Emris, who looked at her almost boyishly. He dropped the lavender to the ground, stuffing his hand back into his pocket.

"You will find Ciro does not take well to orders." He purred, and for a moment, she just stared at him. Ciro had told her he was a conduit, and she had to believe the god.

That explained the glow in his eyes.

She did not hear the god's voice again, but the idea of him still inside her mind made a shiver course down her spine. She met Emris' eyes and knew not if she was speaking to Ciro or him.

"Why didn't you tell me sooner?" She asked, her voice hard. He should have told her before; she thought he was some lunatic. He might as well be.

"And have you dragged me out of your bedroom to be hanged at dawn? Absolutely not," he said, and continued to stroll past her; she followed reluctantly. She had more questions than answers, but it all suddenly made sense. How did he know so much about the gods, and why did he not seem as startled by Morana's voice?

"We have established that I fancy my head." He said, and they passed a servant trimming the bushes. They walked close by and did not resume their conversation until they had walked a far way away. The sun was high in the sky, and a few clouds were visible.

"If I am to pose as your lover, you must make it more believable," he said after a short while. She walked only a few inches away from him, and at his words, stepped further away.

"Why must *I* make it more believable?" He smirked.

"Are you implying that I must chase after you like a love-struck puppy?"

Her silence was enough. She tried to hide the flush in her face, turning to look at a bush of roses very intently.

"Considering that I am a Queen, yes," she said, her face having stopped its insistent burning. He looked shocked for a moment, then offered her his arm.

"Very well then," he said.

They slowly walked back to the palace, and her dread grew more. All the things he had told her threatened her place as Queen. If any servants heard a whisper of their conversations, she would be doomed. And he would no doubt be killed. However, he wasn't her priority; her crown was.

As they were about to part, he leaned down.

"When the shadows start to whisper, come and find me."

With that, he let go of her arm, and she stood there as he walked in silence to his room.

Chapter 15

That night, she sat in her room, huddled in her bed. She could not allow herself to fade into the realm of sleep. Could not allow herself to succumb to a place where Morana might find her. She had asked her servants to bring every candle they could find. Hours later, she sat there in her room, candles illuminating every corner of the space. She kept her eyes open even as darkness engulfed her from outside and her eyelids threatened to close.

She had eaten dinner in her room, not wanting to spend any more time with Emris. He infuriated her, and she wanted nothing to do with him unless necessary.

Her legs were curled into her chest, her arms wrapped around her knees, hair still wet from her bath, clinging slightly to her back. The moon was high in the sky, allowing some light to filter in.

When the shadows start to whisper, come and find me.

His words had unsettled her to the point that she had hastily tracked down all the candles. She had the foolish desire to be with him in the night. Maybe Ciro could silence Morana. But deep down, she knew that Morana had a will of her own. She just hadn't presented herself yet.

The nightmares had stopped since she had stopped sleeping.

Her hands twitched on the blanket as she found herself scanning the room. She hated the thought of the shadows reaching her. Because if everything else he had said was true, then the shadows would call to her. And she did not intend to answer.

Her eyes fluttered shut, and she forced them back open. She tried to keep her mind blank, distract herself with thoughts of Emris, and to infuriate herself. Then, in the corner of the room, a candle flickered out. The windows were all closed, and for a moment, fear gripped Valerie. She slowly stood and lifted a candle from the dresser to relight the one that had been extinguished. As she lit it, another one went out, then another. Until smoke floated up in wisps all around her, she hadn't noticed that it wasn't the wind. No.

It was something else.

Her hands shook as she gripped the candle, her eyes scanning the room. She felt fear coursing through her, and she bent down to light a candle again. After lighting the wick, she did not rise. Instead, she watched. For a few moments, nothing happened, then, as if called to life, a single wisp of darkness curled over the bottom of the candle. She yelped and scurried back, but the wisp did not approach; instead, it strangled the candle and burnt out the small flame.

She was on her feet before she could think, running for her door. Emris had said something like this would happen, and now that it was-

Valerie reached the door, and her hand gripped the knob. The candle in her hands started to flicker with a sudden motion. She turned the knob, but not before the wisp-like ink had crawled across the floor. She tried to move away from it but found herself rooted to the spot.

Her hands shook on the candle, and the wisp neared. She watched as the darkness reached her bare feet and paused as if considering what it was going to do. Before Valerie could move, it crawled up her leg. The sensation was so unnatural that she bucked instinctively, and the wisp clung to her leg like a second skin.

The cold that the darkness brought with it as it crawled up her body was unlike any cold she had ever experienced, as if all warmth had been repelled from its very existence. The wisp slithered up her leg over her skirt, and before she knew it, it curled around her arm. She stood there shaking as the wisp made its way over her wrist. It moved like a snake weaving over her skin, and in one swift motion, it strangled the candle and extinguished the wick.

For a moment, she stood there in complete darkness, fear paralyzing her as she tried to look around the room but found only an unsettling abyss. One that did not exist in the dead of night but was born from something darker. Valerie did not dare call for the guards in the hall; if they saw what she saw, they might turn her right there. She was walking a thin line between her throne and whatever Morana had planned for her.

Valerie stood there frozen as if waiting for something to happen. Then she heard a small voice. It was not one of her dreams of Ciro or even Morana, no. The voice was relatively high-pitched, and it whispered as if alive.

"Who's there?" She called, knowing she shouldn't entertain whatever was lurking in the darkness. As if in answer, a wisp of darkness made its way over the ground. She tried to move out of the way, but it slithered up through the air as if it were a mist, and before she could protest, it twined around her hand.

She shook her hand instinctively, trying to free herself from the shadows.

Foolish girl. Wouldn't you instead ask what is there?

The voice sounded like that of an older woman. That unnerved her. She did not understand what the voice had meant, and then, as if in response, the shadows twined around her fingers, and a voice came from them, once more.

We are shadows.

She let out a strangled yelp, but a tendril of the darkness shot out and clamped a blackened hand over her mouth. Fear filled her eyes, and for a moment, she did not know where to look.

How could this be possible?

It shouldn't be. Shadows did not speak to people.

She shook her head, but the shadow let out a quiet hum.

Shhh, child. It is unwise to scream.

After a moment of terse silence, the darkness withdrew its hand from over her mouth. Her hands were shaking so badly that it felt as if tremors had taken over her whole body. She could barely form words.

"He said this would happen," she breathed, and the wisp cocked its black head as if considering what she had said. A moment later, it withdrew itself from her. She felt the wall behind her breathing intensely, and she squeezed her eyes shut. She tried to convince herself that this was just another dream, that at any moment she would wake up covered in sweat and shaking.

Do you mean Emris?

She dared not respond, letting out a whimper instead. Couldn't the shadows leave her be? After a moment, she opened her eyes and nearly yelped again. The creature sitting a few feet away had green eyes she had seen before. It took her a moment to recognize the pitch-black fur and the tail. Shivers coursed through her body, and bile rose in her throat.

The cat cocked its head, observing her.

It would be wise to answer; you will find I am not as patient as you might assume.

She swallowed, then clamped her hands over her chemise.

"Yes, Emris mentioned you." The cat watched her for another long moment before starting to pad softly to her bed. She found her skin crawling as she watched, fear evident in her body, her heartbeat racing, her palms sweating.

That boy knows nothing of our nature.

The wisps uttered as if trying to convince themselves. The cat jumped nimbly onto the mattress. It settled down as any house cat would and watched her with those emerald green eyes.

The cat from her dreams looked exactly like it. And in that moment, she knew that Morana truly was behind it all. Who would be so cruel as to bring a figment of her night terrors to life? Only a goddess could do it.

"And yet he knew you would come to me," she said, and the cat cocked its head again, eyes narrowing before it licked its paw in a languished manner.

The wisps did not respond, and she dared to take a step closer. A question burned in her mind, and for a moment, she swallowed her fear.

"Are you here to kill me?"

The voice laughed in the air around her, quietly as if amused.

If I wanted to kill you, you would be dead already.

She knew that was true. It did not explain why the cat was still lounging on her bed like a king. She forced herself to walk towards it, aware that at any moment the shadows could come and seize her.

She had to play her cards right. Morana was still unpredictable inside her head, and now the shadows had made their way into her life as well. Both powers were deadly for all she knew. Her head throbbed as she moved towards her bed, her hands clenched into tight fists.

"Why are you here?"

The question sounded silly, but Valerie needed to know. The cat did not look up; instead, its tail flicked lazily in the air.

I am to be your companion.

She felt a flare of anger. Why did everyone seem to want to give the things she had no interest in having? Least of all, a goddess's cruel idea of a companion.

"And what if I find no need for your companionship?" She snapped, and for a moment, she feared the creature might lash out. The cat merely stretched and sat up straighter.

You do not have a say.

She swallowed. Of course, she didn't. "Will you always appear as a cat?" *For the time being.*

"And where will you wander during the day?"

The cat cocked its head once more and licked its paw.

Wherever I feel like.

She bit down on the urge to tell the cat how infuriating it was. But it made sense; if they were truly from Morana and meant to be her companions, they could not be seen in their original form.

Valerie did not sleep. She curled up into the bed, as far away from the cat as she could get, and as her eyes fluttered shut, she had a feeling that something was watching her. She opened her eyes and found the cat staring straight at her.

She huffed a sigh of frustration and turned on her other side. "Would you mind not staring at me?"

I quite like it.

She let out another groan of frustration and pulled the blanket over her head to hide her face from the cat. Whether she wanted to or not, the shadows were finally here. Valerie did not know what they wanted, but she knew exactly who to ask.

Chapter 16

Valerie's nineteenth birthday crept up on her so swiftly that the prospect of holding a gala had not crossed her mind. It wasn't until another council meeting that she was reminded of the fact by Arminia, who had returned from consulting with the commanders in Lunivere and Dramira.

The king and queen had left a few days prior, escorted by some of her finest guards to the border. The prospect of having a gala in celebration of her birth seemed almost cruel. Her mother's mourning had barely commenced.

Nonetheless, she had agreed to let Jezebel come and make her another dress for the gala. Some of the head servants were placed in charge of organizing the throne room into a place suitable for a Cynerian gala. For the past week, servants had bustled in and out of her room, bringing cake samples, colours for tablecloths, and a thousand small things that Valerie knew would make little dent in the gala.

Two days before the gala, she stood in her old room on a small box as Jezebel tested out different fabrics and textures against her skin. For her coronation, she had to wear either blue or silver. But for galas, the royal dressmakers were allowed to express their creativity, although they never strayed far from the royal colours.

Fabrics lay rolled out on the floor; scissors scattered everywhere, and pins pinched fabric together as Jezebel worked in her little world. Valerie stood there silently, not daring to speak words that might derail the seamstress. She had already been waiting nearly half an hour to get an idea of what the dress might be.

What Valerie did not expect was the dark blue fabric, which looked almost black. She stood perfectly still as the seamstress began cutting, folding, and taking measurements.

By the end of their two hours together that morning, Jezebel had picked a style, colour, and shape for the dress. Upon returning to her room, three more servants bustled in concerning invitations. The entire kingdom would be invited, of course, to be the conclusion they reached.

Under her calm facade, Valerie felt her nerves fraying with anxiety.

She had little energy left to worry about such futile things. Yet she couldn't say she was excited about her celebration. She felt too old to spend so much time worrying about a celebration when, in reality, she should be focused on keeping the kingdom running.

Exhaustion weighed on her so heavily that she did not remember climbing into her bed that night. But the dreams - they were indeed something to remember.

Her eyes fluttered open to darkness.

Not the darkness of her room, but of that realm beyond consciousness. Fear seized her immediately as she stood in a black room, and it took her a moment to realize where she was.

The throne room. Her throne room.

Her hands shook slightly as she beheld the room, devoid of any colour, just a shade of black, and when she looked at the throne, she did not see it empty. Her father sat there on the throne.

Months after his death, she had had dreams like this, of him sitting there on the throne. This dream was different.

He sat there wearing the dark blue he had always worn, his brown hair tied back from his face as it always was, broad shoulders square to her. His light blue eyes met hers across the space, and in that moment, she realized it was not her father looking at her.

That's when a slithering feeling crossed her calf; she looked down and saw the black cat once more; its green eyes fixated on a point on the floor as it skipped past her. Her gaze lifted to her father once more. His gaze was stone cold, unflinching, and the sting of sadness hit her square in the chest. She had looked so much like him.

The voice echoed then, cutting through the moment like a dagger.

You never told her, did you, Greyson?

Her stomach churned, and she pinched herself again as she focused on the floor, squeezing her eyes closed as if to coax herself awake.

When she opened them again, the image before her sent her heart racing; her father, with an arrow straight through his throat, was watching her from his throne. She blinked again, tears collecting in the corners of her eyes. The throne was empty then, and for a moment, she had the urge to start running. She did not know where, but fear overtook her every sense.

She blinked again and froze.

The person sitting on the throne was not a face she recognized at first, colder, eyes usually brown, glowing with something unnatural. It took Valerie a moment to pinpoint who it was.

Herself.

Sleep left her.

For the rest of the night, Valerie sat on her balcony staring up at the stars as the soft candlelight burned behind her in the room. She could not bring herself to sit in her bed as if she had not felt her soul tremble at the sight of her father sitting on that throne. Valerie blocked the woman's voice out of her head as best as she could, but the words seemed to be etched into her very chest, unable to depart from her.

Her arms were wrapped around her knees as she rocked back and forth, trying to coax herself back to sleep. Her hands hadn't stopped shaking since she had ripped the blanket off her and vomited in the bathroom basin. Valerie had had enough nightmares in her life to know that this wasn't normal.

Something about the way the voice followed her out of unconsciousness was lost on her. How could it follow her around if it were only a dream?

She stared at the stars, her eyes tracing the different constellations. Her father had always taken pride in his knowledge of the sky, able to name stars off the top of his head and draw constellations with his fingers. Her tutors had never bothered to teach her how to chart the stars, but her father had. She gazed up and saw the raven, curled in the sky, wings stretched wide, and the serpent on its right, three stars over, curling into itself like a conch.

The ocean was still. The moon reflected it almost eerily. When she was younger, she had always believed the merfolk existed, that they lived under the surface of the water, drawing sailors to their ultimate demise. She knew better now than to believe in myths and fairytales.

The only myths that were proven to be real were those of sorcerers and faeries. They were the incarnation of something superior to humans. Conduits - they were unlikely and were the most out-of-the-ordinary thing that humans could understand.

The gods were picky about who they chose as their conduits to live out their rule on their behalf. They rarely picked humans; they wanted the strongest race possible, and, by their reasoning, humans were too weak.

Her hands rubbed warmth back into her arms as she let her chin rest on her knees. Closing her eyes felt traitorous, so she stared out at the ocean, wishing for a saviour that would not come.

Chapter 17

The cat had not followed her down to breakfast. Yet Valerie could still hear the voice of the shadows in her head. Her hands fidgeted with her skirts as she finally sat down at the table, closing her eyes for a moment. When she opened them, she found Emris sitting beside her.

She felt infuriated by the sight of him. Strangely enough, he seemed to have quite a distaste for her as well.

He wore a white button-down that was slightly open, revealing his smooth, muscled chest. The sleeves were rolled up to his elbows, and his black trousers sat low on his hips. His hair, as usual, was unruly and fell around his face, but his eyes were. Those eyes that suddenly made Valerie tighten with rage upon seeing them were the same gold they had been every morning.

If it had not been for Seraphina urging Valerie to at least get clothes brought to him, she would not have allowed her servants to deliver a few trousers, shirts, button-downs, cuffs, and shoes to his room the previous night after dinner. She wouldn't have known after all, since she had been in her room.

103

The two of them sat there in silence for a moment. Valerie fought the urge to snap at Emris for his habit of staring at her.

"I'm assuming you slept horribly," he said, as if he had mentioned something as casual as the weather, and she shot him a glare. She had tossed and turned all night after her encounter with the shadows. Her mind had refused to shut off, with the feeling of those emerald, green eyes staring into her very soul. A shiver raced through her at the thought.

"You assume correctly," she answered, reaching out to sip her water. The corset around her waist pushed her ribs inward at an almost constricting rate.

Emris turned his attention to the knife beside his empty plate. They waited for the servants to bring in the food, and while they did, he spun the knife in his hand. She looked at him as if he were a child.

"Could you not?" She asked, her voice sterner than a lover would address a courtier. Emris didn't stop; instead, he leaned in closer,

"Now why would I stop?"

She felt her jaw clench and the urge to rip the knife from his hand and throw it across the room. Her mind was still whirling from the cat, who had no doubt started to wander around the palace. Could it only hear the shadows? She would find out soon enough.

"Are you always this absurd in the morning, dear?" She bit out, and he caught the word, realizing she was addressing him in his new role—her lover. The knife stopped spinning between his fingers, and he leaned back slightly in his chair, flexing his forearms.

"Only because waking up next to you sparks my need for sarcasm."

Valerie felt the flush on her face, her hands clenching in her skirt. She did not have time for this. She needed to learn more about Morana. Bickering could wait.

She leaned in slightly, and he noticed the serious look in her eyes and dropped his head so he could hear her better.

"You told me to speak with you when the shadows spoke." At that, he let out a small huff of amusement. He leaned in, his voice tickling her ear, and she could smell that fragrance on him once more,

"I'm assuming they have," he purred and leaned in a little more to continue speaking as if he knew the curious ears all over the room were eavesdropping.

"How do they appear?"

She moved back slightly as if to answer him, but the servants entered the room, placing plates of freshly made breakfast in front of them. Valerie focused on the meal, even though her mind was elsewhere. She didn't know if she could trust him, but he was her only way of learning more about what Morana wanted with her.

After they had finished their breakfast, she wiped her mouth with a napkin and rose. His eyes flicked to her, and she fought the urge to flush. His eyes were like pools of molten gold, and they unnerved her as much as they infatuated her.

"Join me?" She asked, and he smiled. Standing swiftly, he held out his arm, and she looped hers through it, brushing the firm muscle of his forearm.

"Always."

As soon as they reached the door to her room, she unhooked their arms. The servants passing by no doubt assumed they were sneaking away to commit unspeakable acts. The door slid open, and for a moment, she felt hopeful. Then she spotted the cat on her windowsill. It was

gazing out at the ocean off in the distance, but upon the door creaking open, it turned.

Emris stepped into the room behind her, and she closed the door, sliding the lock into place. No one could see what had happened because if they did-

"So, this is the way they chose to reveal themselves?" he asked, strolling towards the cat. A few feet away, the cat's back hair stood on end, and it hissed, baring white teeth as its pupils narrowed to slits. In a moment, it jumped off the windowsill and made its way to her bed, watching him from a distance. He seemed to recognize the cat, but then he turned and looked dumbfounded for once.

Valerie nodded, crossing her arms.

"What do you mean by revealing themselves?" Valerie asked, taking a step closer, and the cat, as if sensing her presence, leapt nimbly from the bed, padded over, and curled around her leg. She fought a shiver.

Emris' eyes latched onto the cat and then up her body to her mouth.

"Every conduit god reveals their power through their chosen body. They can manipulate minds into obeying their will. If the conduit is strong enough, they might be able to resist obeying. Some of the gods prefer another way to make sure their conduits obey; they show up in a form." He said, gesturing to the cat still curled around her ankle.

What could Morana want with her?

"Do you have one?" She asked, and Emris nodded, crossing his arms again.

"He usually takes to the sky more often than not." Her steps faltered slightly as she moved away from the cat, who seemed as infatuated with her as Emris was.

"Do they take just one form?" She asked, moving to lean against the wall. He shook his head, moving to the window to gaze out through the gauze.

No. Some gods prefer to stay consistent if they choose to reveal themselves in a physical form other than their conduit. But others vary; many of them decide it based on preference."

The thought sent her hands clenching, jaw tight. That could mean Morana had chosen the cat because of her nightmares. The way it had lingered in her mind.

"Why does she not just speak to me directly then?"

Emris turned back to her, his brow furrowed, looking at her with something resembling frustration.

"That, Valerie, is something I do not know."

Her heart plummeted. How was he supposed to help her if he did not even know why Morana refused to speak to her the way Ciro talked to him? Anger flared in her chest, and she pointed a finger at the door,

"Get out," she said, and Emris turned to her again, shocked almost beyond words. "Valeri-"

"I said, get out." She could not wrap her mind around how he was just as clueless as she was. It was impossible. He did not move from where he stood, she did not stalk towards him, but she had the urge to strike him more than she ever had. He knew nothing. The shadows had been right; he knew nothing.

"You claim to know so much about Morana, but you are just as clueless as I am," she whispered loudly. If anyone overheard, questions might be asked. Her advisors had already begun to grow paranoid about her lack of effort in responding to their tedious requests.

Emris took a step forward; his eyes narrowed slightly on her. She feared he would strike her, and for a moment she flinched.

"Do you think me rash enough to strike a woman?" He asked, and a flush crept up her face. He observed her for another moment before finally sighing.

"I do not know why Morana has not spoken to you, and if she has, I cannot explain it either. Morana is a goddess of deception; one moment, she is stable, the next irrational."

Emris explained this as he walked over to the cat, still lounging on the bed. As if demonstrating his point, he reached out and petted the cat's sleek black fur. It purred into his hand. Minutes ago, it had hissed at him like a threat, and now-

Valerie found her head spinning, her hand gripped her bedpost, and she sighed.

"None of this makes any sense," she murmured under her breath. Emris hummed in agreement. She cast a sidelong glance at him to find him still petting the cat.

"Why do you want to hear from Morana?" She asked, she had never asked him his motive for wanting to speak with the goddess or at least hear her voice. He tensed slightly, his hand stilling on the cat. For a moment, she expected him to surrender finally, telling her it was all a scheme to murder her, but instead, he simply turned around to face her.

"We must all succumb to the will of the gods," he uttered casually.

"Are you saying Ciro wants to speak with her?" she replied.

Emris examined his hand for a moment and then nodded.

"Can't they just speak to each other in a different place then?" She asked, and he let out a small laugh once more. He rubbed his nose with his index finger and thumb as if to ease a migraine.

"The gods do not speak to each other at all, Valerie. They find no need to communicate. Ciro wants to speak with Morana through me," he said, and she cocked her head, furrowing her brow in question.

"Morana is a rash goddess; the other gods fear her, even Ciro. If he went to her in the Realm Above, she could have him eternally destroyed." He said as if telling a folktale to small children.

"So, you are the messenger?"

"In short, yes." He responded. He slowly walked forward, and she did not step back this time. She felt thunder with her heartbeat; she still couldn't understand all of this. There was something he refused to tell her.

"That is why you need to be on your guard," he said as if in warning. A shiver ran down her spine.

"Why?"

"Because if I make one wrong move, Morana will kill you." As soon as the words left his mouth, she stumbled back. Her hand flew to her lips. She couldn't believe it. She stumbled back farther and hit a vase, which was shattered on the ground. She swore.

Her hands were shaking, and when Emris stepped forward, her hand shot out.

The shadows had spoken to her about him, not in detail, but she knew that they had something against him that she did not know.

"You're here to kill me," she said softly, and she ran to her door. She did not care if they executed her; he would kill her; Morana would kill her. Before she could reach the handle, he was across the room, his hand over her mouth, and he pulled her back against his chest. The firm muscles pressed flush against her back, and she writhed, trying to claw his hand from her mouth. The cat turned on the bed, hissing once more, but Emris did not budge.

"I am not here to kill you, I am here to help you," he said.

She whimpered against his hand.

His one arm was wrapped around her waist, firmly pulling her back against his chest.

Fear coursed through her, and in that moment, all rationality left her. Without thinking, she slammed the bottom of her heel into his foot; his arm loosened slightly as he grunted, but his hand remained on her mouth. She slammed her elbow back into his ribcage, but he only grunted. She got free from his grasp for a moment, and before she knew it, she ran towards the bed.

"Valerie, listen to me," he said and stalked towards her as she reached for the dagger on her bedside, holding it between them. He raised his hands slightly.

"We have already come to this conclusion," he said, almost mockingly, and took another step forward.

"Have you no trust in me? I have warned you about the Shadows, and they spoke to you, did they not?" he said, and he gestured to the cat, which was still hissing from behind her.

Her hands were not shaking around the blade.

She glared at him, eyes flicking from his hands to his golden eyes.

"Stay away," she said, and the cat hissed once more in unison with her. His mouth quivered with a smirk, as if her life was funny, sometimes to gamble away.

"You said yourself that one wrong move from you and Morana would kill me," she said, taking another step back. One of the servants must have heard the vase crash; they would come to check on her soon.

"You have to trust-"

Before he could finish the sentence, pain flared behind her eyes so brightly that she staggered again. Her hands shook around the blade, but she kept it up; she would not drop her guard, least of all now. The smirk vanished from his face and was replaced by concern. He took a step forward, reaching for her elbow, and she felt her vision blurring. She did not know what was happening. The tremors started so violently in her hands that for a moment she could not stop them. With a painful gasp, she dropped the dagger.

"Valerie," he said firmly as if trying to coax her out of something; she could not breathe for a moment. Her eyes could not focus. He swore and surged forwards, not minding the cat that was hissing profusely.

She did not see the glow in his palm until a voice echoed in her head. It was not Shadow. No, it was Morana. She did not see the glow in his palm until a voice echoed in her head. It was not the shadows. No, it was Morana.

Valerie.

Chapter 18

Darkness was thicker than anything she had ever seen surrounding her. She tried to move but found that her eyes were the only part of her that would open. Her legs felt stiff, and for a moment she feared she was dead, that Morana had truly grown tired of the games.

Behind her, she heard banging. Slowly, she rose from the ground, which was covered in water. She did not sink. She had not been in the realm of dreams in days.

She could not see where the sound came from, only that it did not stop, even as Morana stepped into the space.

It was as if the entirety of the space was humming when she stepped into it. She did not appear like the cat. Did not shield her appearance from Valerie. Her hands shook as she fully beheld the goddess.

Her skin was the whiteness of a corpse, yet some colour was in her cheekbones, a darker shade of white that outlined her high jawline and cheeks. Her eyes were dark green, slit, and focused entirely on her. She stood only a few inches taller than Valerie, and yet she still found herself stumbling back. A dark dress clung to her body, not deteriorating as a corpse might. She was beautiful. Hauntingly so.

No wonder she drove her former conduits mad.

Her hands were dark, slowly fading into the whiteness of the rest of her skin. Her black hair fell down her back, straight. For a moment, they just stood there staring at each other. Then she spoke.

"Hello, Valerie." She said her voice could tear the hearts out of men's bodies and stop their lungs from breathing. For a moment, fear coursed so vividly through Valerie that she thought she might die right there. Morana cocked her head slightly as if observing her. She understood why Morana used a cat to show herself; she moved like one, lithe and powerful.

Valerie felt her mouth dry up, unable to form words. What would she say? What was there to say? Morana had imprisoned her inside her mind.

"Are you not going to welcome me?" The goddess asked, stepping closer slowly, and as if in tandem, Valerie took a step back. Morana clicked her tongue slightly in a tsk.

"There is no need to cower, child," she said, and before Valerie could blink, Morana was at her ear. She stood behind Valerie, her hands on Valerie's shoulders, and it felt as if she was touched by death itself. In that moment, Valerie swallowed and forced herself to form words.

"What do you want from me?" she asked, and Morana laughed darkly in her ear as if surprised by her lack of knowledge. For a moment, she could not see the goddess. She spun around to look for her but found nothing.

"What I want from you will be revealed in time. For now, I want you to listen." Morana purred as she appeared once more on a throne made from bones. Valerie felt bile rise in her throat.

"Kneel."

Morana's voice came out deeper than usual. Without knowing what came over her, Valerie fell to her knees as if commanded. She tried to stand, but couldn't.

"Do you see what I can do? I can tell you to kneel or slit your own throat, and you would do it without hesitation," Morana said softly, watching as Valerie stared at the ground with tears in her eyes. What had she done to deserve this?

"You will find that I do not take betrayal lightly," she said, as if she knew what Valerie wished deep inside her soul, that she wanted Morana gone. "You have no power, but I will give you unimaginable sovereignty, Valerie, if you obey me. She said, and Valerie had the urge to cry out, but found that her mouth was shut, as if she were unable to open it. The slamming continued far off in the distance, and for a moment, Morana's eyes lingered on Valerie before flicking to a space far behind her. She chuckled to herself. "It seems he is trying to get in." At the words, Valerie tensed. Was she speaking of Emris? If she were, why hadn't she just killed her?

"Ciro does not know how to keep his boy on a leash."

Valerie suddenly was afraid, not for herself, but for Emris. If he died, she would be left alone with Morana, no one to confide in, no one to ask.

"Here is your first order," she said, and Valerie stopped breathing. She tried to shut her mind out, but found there was no place to hide from Morana and her will. She was a puppet, and she could not disobey a god.

Morana smiled softly, and it was the most haunting thing Valerie had ever seen. Morana stepped forward and placed a hand on Valerie's head before tilting her chin upwards. Tears blurred her eyes, and she could barely see the goddess's face.

She then realized that Morana was merely smiling. "Do not cry, child," she said softly, and, as if betraying herself, her body stopped producing tears. She stared at the goddess with as much hatred as she could muster, only to find that Morana was smiling.

She leaned forward and pressed her mouth against Valerie's ear.

Wake.

The space disappeared around her as she drowned in the water once more.

Chapter 19

Emris watched as Valerie awoke from the realm. His arms were around her, and he cradled her head in his arms as if she were something precious. She had pointed a knife at him. Again.

He knew Morana had pulled her under; he had summoned Ciro moments before she had been pulled away, catching her before she slammed into the ground.

The barrier between his mind and hers had stood firm, like iron walls that he had slammed against until his knuckles were bruised.

Valerie stirred in his arms, and her eyes flew open moments later, gasping as if she had been underwater. He immediately urged her to sit up, and she grasped his shirt out of instinct. She was looking around the room in fear. He knew that fear, the kind that stayed in your stomach no matter what. The type that followed you in and out of unconsciousness. The fear of uncertainty.

"Valerie, look at me," he said and grasped her shoulders slightly. He noticed then that her eyes were tear-stained.

Gods, what had Morana said to her?

"Don't touch me, don't…" she said, crying, still as if he were Morana. But he knew she feared him. He had nearly stopped breathing when she had collapsed and assumed that Morana had finally killed her. Decided she was not worth it for Emris to bother continually. It had nearly killed him, and he couldn't say why.

"Look at me," he said more firmly and caught her hands. Her brown eyes met his; they seemed broken.

His eyes softened instinctively. He had known conduits like her before. Upon entering the presence of their god, they always came out changed. Emris had.

He had vomited for hours after meeting Ciro for the first time. He knew what the gods did to the minds of mortals. Knew and saw it in her eyes.

"Did she hurt you?" He demanded his gut clench as he examined her face for any harm.

She shook her head, still shaking, and for a moment, she could barely seem to stop crying. He did not wipe away her tears; he did not try to tell her she would be alright. He could not guarantee that.

He had nearly caused her death.

Ciro wanted to speak to Morana. His mental shield was up when he was around her, because Morana had been trying to break his mental barricade down for days and crept up on him to get to Ciro.

He barely slept.

But he could not seem to get Valerie out of his head. And that was a dangerous thing.

"What did she say to you?" He asked if Morana could have told her anything. Things that he had not said, things he did not want to say.

Valerie backed away from him, pushing away until her back hit her bed. Her arms wrapped around her knees. Hands still shaking.

She shook her head, staring at him as if he were not there. Her usually fiery eyes were filled with blunt terror. The kind that killed.

The cat did not hiss again; instead, it had scurried across the room to play with a shard of the broken vase. He sat where he was, not wanting to startle her more than she already was. The terror would fade, and then she would be back to herself. He hated that fear crept into his chest. He schooled his features. He was good at it, but underneath the surface, a storm was raging.

"You…you tried to get to me," she said softly, then her eyes flicked to meet his, and he stopped breathing. He had.

He had followed her to the edge of the realm, had slammed himself against the barricade, trying to get to her. He didn't know why he had done it. Morana could have killed him while he was there.

He tightened his hand into a fist.

"I did," he said softly, and for a moment she stopped crying; those fierce eyes that always stared at him with hatred softened ever so slightly. Her gaze flicked down to his hand, which was heavily bruised.

"You were the one slamming against the barricade." "I was," she confirmed his suspicion.

Her eyes flickered with something that might have been shocked, but as she opened her mouth to say something, someone knocked on the door—then entered.

The two of them were sitting there on the floor, a vase broken, and she was crying. Seraphina was immediately on guard, her hand on her sword as she crossed the room. She grasped him by the arm and yanked him upwards,

"What did you do?" She demanded, looking down at Valerie, who was still curled on the floor. Guilt clawed at his chest, but he levelled his gaze at the guard.

"I found her like this," he lied, and his eyes flicked to Valerie. Seraphina spun around to look at Valerie again, her peripheral vision on him still. Valerie looked between them and nodded. She lied to him.

I'll find a servant to clean up the vase," she said and made her way over to the scraps. Upon seeing the cat, she startled slightly.

"Is he one of the servants?" Seraphina asked, but Valerie sat there shaking, unable to move. He stepped in front of her, slightly shielding her from Seraphina's gaze. She could be unstable; Morana could lash out at her at any moment.

"I got him as a gift for Her Majesty's birthday," he said, and Seraphina looked skeptically at him before nodding. She then left the room, murmuring something to a servant in the hall. Whether she knew they were 'lovers,' he was unsure.

As soon as the door shut, he turned back to Valerie. She was sitting there rocking back and forth on the floor. He wavered for only a moment before he moved to her side, kneeling. He lifted her into his arms, and she tensed for a moment instinctively, then relaxed slightly, still in shock, her eyes fixed on a point far away.

He lifted her easily; her body cradled against him as he slowly moved them to the bed. He set her down on the covers. Making sure that the servant wasn't about to enter, he slipped into his mind.

He rarely asked Ciro for anything, but he knew she would break down if he did not do something to ease her.

After a few moments, his hand glowed as it had when he had chased her unconsciously. Slowly, he met her eyes and moved his hand, and she inched away.

"It will help," he said, and she stared at him for a moment before she closed her eyes slightly. Slowly, he pressed his index finger to her temple. He had used his ability to make a dream come true. An exquisite dream.

Ciro was the god of light and visions. Emris never slept because he always dreamed, some dreams more unsettling than others. He did everything he could to escape them. He knew she needed something else. Slowly, her eyes fluttered closed, and he sat beside the bed for a moment. He had crafted a dream of an ocean, of ships and shells and beautiful whales. Her face relaxed slightly as the dream filled her mind. He sat for a moment before he made his way to the balcony doors, opening them in one smooth motion. The air filled the room, carrying a cool breeze that dried her tears. With a glance back at her, he stepped onto the balcony.

His head was throbbing, and his hands ached.

The ocean air filled his nose, and he gazed out at the water, watching ships enter and leave the harbour. He stayed there for a long moment, gazing out at Linra, the beautiful oceanside kingdom.

Morana would destroy it, no doubt. She always did. Emris wanted to tell Valerie, but it would spell doom for both.

The cat had made its way onto the balcony beside him and swiftly jumped onto the stone railing. Even now, Morana was watching over them through those green eyes. Something bitter curled in his chest, and he fiddled with his sleeve.

The cat did not move closer but seemed to be gazing out at the view as well. He weighed what he was about to do and turned his head; the cat did not acknowledge him, but he knew it was listening.

"If Morana hurts her, it will spell her doom," he said, his voice filled with something akin to anger.

The cat merely turned its head, and its mouth stretched into a small smile.

Chapter 20

Valerie did not remember waking up, only that it was for the first time in weeks. Upon awaking, her hands were slightly curled around the blanket, hair strewn on the pillow beside her. She had dreamed of beautiful things that had long since left her mind.

Oceans and seas, beautiful creatures, her ship. Things that in another life would have brought her endless joy. Were it not for the memory of Morana, she would have awoken peacefully. The interaction had left her so shocked that she didn't remember much of what happened after she awoke from the trance—she hadn't remembered anything other than Emris.

You tried to get to me. I did.

The words sent a flush to her cheeks. It had not hit her then what it meant for him to come looking for her. Why? Everything about Emris was a mystery. She sat up, her head spinning as she let her legs dangle off the side of the bed. The dreaded cat sat on the chair by the bed, asleep. The sun was setting, and she assumed the dream with Morana had taken place a few hours prior. The vase that had shattered on the ground had been cleaned, leaving the white marble floor unmarred. It took her a moment to realize that Seraphina stood by the balcony doors, gazing out at the setting sun.

She turned and caught Valerie's eye. She had questions, Valerie knew. She had not had time to explain entirely; he was her lover. For a moment, it seemed as if Seraphina did not know where to look. Valerie set up straighter, running her hand through her curls. How would she explain this to Seraphina? How could she justify the appearance of a lover suddenly?

Seraphina approached the bed slowly. For a moment, she looked at Valerie, still trying to see what was wrong. The cat did not stir from its position on the chair, and Valerie hoped foolishly that it would stay asleep for the time being. Her head throbbed insistently, and she savoured the quiet before Seraphina spoke.

"How do you know the man?" she asked, her voice curious. This was not a commander asking her queen for instructions; this was a friend consulting with her dearest acquaintance. At that moment, Valerie had the urge to confess everything that had happened. She cleared her throat to hide the burning behind her eyes. She wanted to tell her friend everything she'd never kept a secret from her, and doing so now was wrong. But she knew that telling her the truth would only result in a horrible fate for her and Emris.

"Do you promise not to tell the other advisors?"

The question might've sounded silly, but she needed to be sure Seraphina wouldn't spread more court rumours. There was no doubt that she had taken a lover; the servant had a habit of gossiping. Seraphina nodded, then her gaze turned serious as she fixed her eyes on Valerie once more.

"What's going on, Valerie?" she asked more seriously. Valerie took a moment to school her features, making it appear as if there wasn't a storm raging behind her calm face. Morana's voice still throbbed behind her eyes, and she couldn't stop herself from squeezing the linens between her hands.

"The man, his name is Emris."

Valerie started. She sat there for a moment, trying to piece together the story that she was crafting on the spot. But sitting there now under her friend's gaze, eyes she could not remember, the carefully crafted tale she had woven.

"A few months ago, before-"

Her voice broke off; she did not know how to speak of her mother's death still, but she forced herself to level Seraphina a glance that said enough. Her friend nodded as if in understanding.

"I was at the market while my mother was busy speaking with advisors."

That part was genuine. Seraphina knew her mother had been busy speaking to advisors constantly, never taking the time to talk to her daughter unless it was concerning her tutoring or training, as if she were nothing more than another sentinel under her command.

"I had wandered into a small bakery," she waved her hand slightly as if to recall the memory. "You know the one on the corner by the harbour," she said, and Seraphina nodded, remembering all the times they had strolled there together while the queen had forgotten about Valerie.

"Well, this was a day when you weren't there," she said, and she could see the shock on Seraphina's face. There had been many times when she had not gone anywhere with Seraphina, least of all to the town. Around the full-moon ceremony, the Priestesses often announced to the people, which sparked many festivals featuring all sorts of finery, from baking competitions to vendors selling foreign wares on the streets. Seraphina seemed to try to recall a memory that did not come to her. Valerie feared she had drawn herself into a trap.

"It was while you were away last summer during your campaign with General Arminia," she said, her voice wavering slightly, but Seraphina nodded, nonetheless. She had gone for nearly three months on the campaign to the wall, and part of Valerie knew that Seraphina would never forgive herself for leaving for so long.

For a moment, the two of them just stared at each other. Seraphina watched her as she waited for her to continue. Valerie stood then, as if to bring life to the conversation once more. She ignored the way her head throbbed and the way she lost her footing slightly as she stood. The cat did not stir on the chair.

"Well, you see, the baker has a nephew from Jamiah, and I was rather taken with him."

At the word, Seraphina cocked her brow; her mother had always been strict about what she expected for Valerie's life; the entire palace knew that she was to be wed to one of the Noble Human kings or princes rather. This was new information, and Valerie found it easier to lie to her now than to express the truth that she did not want to marry a royal.

"We spoke once or twice and-"

She broke off her thought, forcing herself to remember a timid moment. She forced herself to blush as if she were flustered, her hands clenched, and Seraphina gave her a look. She did not expect her friend to understand romance at all; she was bred of blood and war; she did not understand what it was to love. No. Valerie knew that wasn't true. Seraphina had loved, or at least if she had, she had never spoken to Valerie about it explicitly. Seraphina loved it very much. It was her only weakness.

Valerie schooled her features once more but turned to the balcony as if to draw more thoughts.

"You see," she said, "I had told him that I would've loved to see him again, and well, he said that he would have loved to court me if it wasn't for my mother and all the preparations for the possible war," she said, her hands fisting together in front of her torso.

She could barely breathe. It felt as if lying were slowly constricting her, and she couldn't stop; if she stopped now, Seraphina would see that something was wrong, and she would be exposed.

"Oh, Seraphina," she said softly as if about to break into tears. Her friend immediately approached her. "When I saw him again at the ball, I could not resist him."

"Valerie," Serphina said. "I understand, truly I do, but you must be careful, now that your mother is gone, there's no one to protect you from threats other than your advisors and me. You must promise me, Valerie, that you will not give your heart away easily; it is a precious thing. "

Valerie found herself blinking back real tears.

Her heart had never been marvelled over; no one had ever taken the time to see her in her darkest moments. Her mind flashed back to Emris, who had cradled her in his arms when she had awoken from the realm. It sent pain through her gut, and for a moment, she found the lie not so unbelievable. Seraphina smiled softly, as if remembering now that her friend was awake and safe. She placed a gentle hand on Valerie's shoulder, the weight of the armour sinking into her skin.

"I'm glad you're alright," she said softly.

Then she drew back as if slipping into that cold gaze of a guard. It stung slightly whenever Valerie had to watch the shift, but she knew that, as Seraphina had to shift into the armour, she had to change into the crown. How long had the advisors been searching for her? They no doubt wondered what happened to her. It no longer mattered; all that mattered was that Seraphina believed her fully.

"I must go Arminia insists that we circle back to the border. I will be gone for a few days."

She made her way to the door, but not before hugging her friend tightly. She whispered in her ear softly enough for a moment, and the world stilled.

"Take care of yourself, Valerie."

It was the hardest thing to remember what had happened the last time Sera was gone on a campaign. She had lost her mother. Seraphina still blamed herself for not staying, insisting that if she had been there, none of it would have happened and that Valerie would not have been left to carry the burden of so many dead kings. She hugged her friend back,

"You as well, Seraphina, and thank you for understanding."

Her friend pulled away, and she almost saw tears glitter in her eyes. She nodded to her friend, who bowed, then she slipped out of the room. Just as she left, the cat yawned awake, and for a moment, Valerie realized lying to Seraphina had been the hardest thing she had ever had to do.

When she saw Emris at dinner, his eyes were ashen as if he hadn't slept. He sat beside her, and upon meeting her eyes, a slight smirk twitched on his lips. She remembered how he had cradled her against his chest, whispered words that now seemed foolish-

"How are you feeling?" He asked softly, his voice interrupting her thoughts. She swallowed, then levelled him with a soft gaze. As if not expecting it, he cocked a brow.

"Better, thank you for earlier," she said softly. The servants no doubt thought they were lovers. If they did not assume anything else, she would accept the title of his lover.

Emris froze for a moment between bites of his egg. He met her eyes and, for a moment, another emotion lingered there.

"You're welcome," he purred softly. She met his eyes again, and her heartbeat sped up. She could not forget Morana's words in the back of her head, and yet she could not forget how he had so fiercely tried to take care of her. The feelings mixed in her chest, and as much as she tried to decipher them, she found it nearly impossible to decide what she felt. Her advisors had informed her that there was another meeting the next day. She didn't know if she could trust Emris to keep himself occupied.

A servant slowly made their way to the table, bowing low before addressing Valerie directly.

"Your Majesty, a letter from Dramira."

Valerie's eyes widened slightly, and she nodded before taking the envelope from the girl's hand, who bowed again quickly and scurried off. For a moment, she just sat there weighing the envelope in her hand. Emris seemed to pause, watching her as if she were a mystery.

"Are you going to open it?" He asked softly, placing his knife and fork down.

Valerie didn't respond for a moment, her head aching once more. Then she nodded and slowly turned it over. She broke open the red seal and pulled the paper out. She seemed to hold her breath for a moment. She read the contents, hands shaking around the corners of the paper:

Dearest Queen Valerie Denisera

Although I wished to have attended your recent birthday celebration, I was held back by many formal meetings. Nonetheless, I am writing to establish a formal desire to court you. I genuinely hope to see you soon. Please consider my offer.

Prince Castiler

Her hands shook around the paper once more, and she found her eyes blurring. If she married him, she would be making him king; she would lose her power over her kingdom and hand it to him on a silver platter. If she did not, he might refuse to ally with her in case of a war.

She did not notice the shadows that curled under her ankles under the table. But Emris did. Acting swiftly, he moved his hand and rested it on hers.

Valerie did not flinch at the touch; instead, she faced him, his hand firm around hers. His eyes flicked down for a moment, and upon seeing the shadows, she relaxed. She still had no control over them, but her calming down seemed to soothe the darkness.

"What does it say?" He asked softly, his thumb running over the back of her hand. To all the guards around the room, it was established that they were lovers. The guise was slowly knitting itself together, but this - this would ruin it with court gossip and tales of the presumptuous queen of Cyneria.

"Could we retire?" She asked, her gaze flicking down to her skirt, trying to stop the tears that filled her eyes. Softly, she blinked them away, but upon seeing his eyes, he gave a nod. He pushed away from the table and extended his arm to her. She took the letter in her other hand and hooked her arm on his.

They reached her room minutes later. She went inside and quietly shut the door. Emris let go of her arm almost instantly, and for a moment she stood there with her fists balled. Then her gaze fixed on Emris. Something had softened in his features, only to harden again. He wore his white, ruffled shirt with brown trousers and shoes that were slightly undone.

He looked as beautiful as he always did in the moonlight.

Anger boiled in her gut at the letter, and she threw it down to the floor in a fit of frustration. She started to busy herself with anything else. She started to undress herself. Her shoes came off first, then she pulled off her pearl necklace and set it down on her dresser, then her hair came down from its braid.

Emris had made his way to the letter and picked it up. She did not dare hold her breath while he read it. He gave a small chuckle, and she nearly whirled around. Instead, she glared at him in the mirror.

"What could be entertaining about this?" She demanded her hands, shaking as she reached back, trying to undo her tight corset. The blue fabric is clinging to her like a second skin.

"He does not seem to be a poet," he said

She managed to get the first bow loose, but pulling the strings seemed rather complicated. A servant helped her pull it tight every morning, but now it seemed almost impossible to do. She refused to ask him for help and continued to struggle for a few minutes.

"Do you need me to help?" he asked, and for once, she scoffed. She turned to meet his eyes.

"You wouldn't know how to undo a corset unless I gave you instructions," she quipped, her frustration boiling over into her voice. Everything in her life was going wrong. If she did not agree to her union with Castlier, she would be doubted by her advisors. Questions would be asked. Providing horrible questions that would lead to her being exposed.

He merely smirked, a small huff of a laugh escaping him.

"You would be surprised, Sweetheart, it is one of my many talents."

"What, undoing corsets or following instructions?" She quipped, even though her face had flushed red.

"You love to oppose me."

"And you love to infuriate me."

He took a few steps closer and slowly untangled her fingers from the corset back. She did not fight him, although she stopped breathing. Slowly, he pulled on each string. Finally, the bodice collapsed, and she could finally breathe again. He stepped back, and his warmth left with him.

"Are you going to court him?" He asked with his hands in his pockets. Something foolish inside of her wanted to say no, but she knew better. She moved to the other side of the room behind the dressing screen. She shifted out of the sleeves, then the corset, leaving her in only her underwear, the entire time she had the feeling he could see through the screen. Her cheeks flushed.

She pulled on a white nightgown, and for a moment she feared it would be too revealing.

"Turn around," she said, and for a moment there was stillness.

"Do you think I will leer at you, Your Majesty?" He mocked, and for a moment, she considered shoving her dagger into his spine.

"Do it," she said, and for a moment she paused. Then he sighed. "As you wish," he murmured. "Do it," she said, and for a moment she waited. Then he sighed. "As you wish," he murmured.

After a few more seconds, she peeked away from behind the screen. He had indeed turned around, facing the door, hands in his pockets still. She quickly glanced down at herself, and then she made her way to the bed, practically bolting. No man had ever seen her in her nightgown. And she didn't intend to let anyone know. As soon as she had climbed under the covers, she cleared her throat.

Slowly, he turned, and his breath seemed to catch. She had never felt beautiful in her life, never felt even worthy of a smile, but as his eyes raked over her for a moment, he seemed at a loss for words.

"I don't have a choice in the matter of allowing him to court me," she said, changing the subject, and he blinked as if leaving a daze.

He met her eyes, and then he ran a hand through his white hair, those dimples coming alive again.

"Why is that?" He asked, and for a moment, she truly believed he was messing with her. Did he not know the pressure she was under? Understand that if she denied the prince, she would be dooming both her and her kingdom.

"I do not have to explain my choices to you," she snapped, and for a moment, she feared her temper had gotten the best of her. But his eyes remained soft, and she felt a guilty flare in her gut.

"I'm assuming not many men have asked for the privilege of courting you?"

She felt indignation flare in her chest. Was he calling her ugly? Her eyes hardened, and in that moment, she realized he was just like every other man.

"I cannot say that many have." "Is he your first?"

She nodded. Her mouth closed as she chewed on her lip. His eyes softened once more.

"Are all men in Cyneria fools?" He asked, stepping closer to the bed, and he loomed over the bed, and for a moment, she remembered where they were, how dark the room was.

"Why would you ask that?" She questioned, brow furrowing as she wrapped her hands around the silken sheets.

"You have no idea?" He asked, almost shocked, and she just stared at him.

Without saying another word, he walked to the balcony door, hand hovering over the handle.

"They must all be fools, because if anyone saw you for more than a moment in time, they would be utterly infatuated with you."

She felt her heart stutter in her chest. He couldn't mean it. They were nothing more than mutual conduits, each seeking the same goal. Both were tied to Morana.

"Are you implying I am beautiful, Emris?" She asked his name, rolling off her lips. He tensed for a moment and ran a hand through his hair once more. Her heart thundered, and she dreaded what he would answer, feared he would turn it into some joke.

"You are captivating."

The statement felt so sure, as if he knew her personally. For a moment, the room held its breath, and a flush crept up her cheeks. The cat, which had been somewhere in the corner, finally made its way over to them and jumped onto the chair beside the bed.

Emris took that as his sign.

"Would you like another dream?" He asked softly as if to avoid the cat hearing him. Her heart stuttered again. She remembered now that he had given her the lovely dream. It seemed almost too good to be true.

He was offering so much, something she had not had in a while. She nodded nonetheless, and he approached the bed, hands still in his pockets. He stopped inches away from her then, and instead of looming over her, he dropped to a knee beside the bed, his eyes meeting hers for a moment. His eyes flicked down to her lips and then back to her eyes. She lost her breath.

"What is your favourite colour?" He asked softly, and she noticed that his left index finger had started to glow; his eyes remained fixed on her face as if she were an altar.

She thought for a moment. No one had ever asked her. In a kingdom where blue was the most common, and it was the only colour she wore more than others, she had never really taken the time to learn from the others. For a moment, she stopped breathing, closed her eyes, and as if a traitor had entered her mind, one word stood out.

Gold.

Not the gold of an altar or necklaces but the gold of his eyes. For a moment, she reconsidered.

"Red," she murmured, but he only smirked. He leaned in so that his breath tickled her ear, and for a moment she felt as if time slowed down.

"Sweetheart, you know better than to lie," he whispered, and his finger touched her temple. She faded into unconsciousness, and in the dream, she did not see red. Instead, she saw gold.

Chapter 21

Emris watched as the dream took shape within her mind. He knelt there beside the bed for a moment, his finger lingering on her temple before he slowly pulled back. He had seen in her eyes that she was lying; it had just been a lucky guess to see if she had picked a colour.

Emris hated his eyes. They had glowed after he was born, once russet hazel, now a glowing gold that contrasted with his tanned skin and snow-white hair. He gazed at Valerie for a moment, his eyes still soft.

He had seen the anger in her upon reading the letter, had seen how a part of her recoiled at the thought of being courted. Whether that was in general or just concerning the prince, he did not know.

Emris traced her freckles with his eyes, her curls slightly messy against the silk. Her brow, which was usually furrowed when she looked at him, was relaxed; her lips were slightly parted in sleep. Her fingers curled loosely around the blanket, her white nightgown clinging to her body, and a strap hanging somewhat off one shoulder.

Gods, she was beautiful.

His jaw clenched. He had seen the raw surprise inside her eyes upon his calling her captivating. Emris had told himself he found her nothing more than another woman, that she was not even attractive.

He lied.

Slowly, he rose, gazing down at her, and then at the cat still on the chair. Without a second glance, he left her room, shutting the door quietly behind him. Whenever he gave her a dream, Morana would not be able to reach her, at least not for a while. Ciro had given him that power.

He knew the goddess would be furious if he had diverted Valerie away from her.

But he did not think about it.

When he finally arrived in his room, he sat on the bed, his elbows on his knees. He did not dream, even if he wanted to. Ciro only gave him occasional visions, and when he didn't, he slept as if dead. The dreams he crafted were transferred to others. He rubbed his index and thumb together.

As if to recall how her soft skin had felt under his touch.

His jaw clenched slightly. How did she not notice? Emris had seen gods face-to-face, enchantresses, faeries, and sorceresses. He had stared into the eyes of thousands of women, but every single pair paled in comparison to *hers*.

He closed his eyes with a sigh as if to remember her face carved into his mind. Since that night at the gala with her in his arms, he could not get those brown eyes out of his mind. Could not flee from them in sleep or consciousness.

He realized that he could stare into her eyes for hours without growing tired. That was dangerous. His hands flexed on his knees.

Attraction was dangerous. It pulled people away from their purpose. His lips quivered into a soft smirk.

She followed him around like a curse, her eyes, her laugh, her goddamned voice sent him on edge. She was a mystery that he could not unravel, not because of Morana, far from it.

Because Valerie was something he had never been allowed to want.

That night, when he closed his eyes, it was not Ciro who visited him. Morana stepped into his mind like a predator. Emris knew her voice, and yet when she spoke, he froze where he sat on the ground in the darkness.

"You are a foolish boy," she purred, and Emris let out a tight breath. He had faced her before, but this was different. She seemed angry. Very few saw Morana angry and survived telling the tale.

"First you threaten me," she said, stepping closer, and he shivered as one of her hands drifted through his hair, stroking his scalp as one would a hound. "And now you give her dreams."

Her hands slipped from his hair, and he could feel the raw anger in her voice. In the silence that followed. If she wanted to kill him, she could. Ciro could not protect him if she were in his mind. For a moment, he feared she would kill him right there, but she merely sat down on a throne a few feet away, one that had not been there moments before.

"Do you have a death wish?" She asked him, her nails running over the armrest. Emris smirked softly as if he were not sitting in front of the goddess of death. Before he could answer, she was in front of him with a hand gripping his jaw as he had gripped Valerie's days ago. He felt that fear as her emerald-green eyes bore into him; he could not look away.

She leaned carefully.

"You may give her false hope, boy, but if you ever touch her again, I will gut you and keep you alive long enough to apologize." She whispered, and he felt his heartbeat skyrocket. When Morana made threats, they were not whimsical; they were promises.

He did not have time to blink before he fell through the floor.

He did not remember waking, only that when he did, the cat was sitting in his room, tail flicking lazily.

Part 2

Chapter 22

Valerie sat at the council table; dread coiled so deeply in her gut she couldn't breathe. Emris had not appeared at breakfast, nor had she sent for him. What if Morana, furious about the dreams, had decided to kill him? Could Ciro protect him?

The cat had not been in her room when she had awoken. Her hands shook slightly as she fisted them in her skirt.

Callus sat to her right; his eyes fixed on a spot on the table. As Seraphina had told her, Arminia was at the wall once more. She did not doubt her advisor's judgement. She had protected Cyneria by taking the offensive; if she had to miss a council gathering, then so be it.

As her mind remained fixed on Emris, Dimitrius cleared his throat as if trying to draw her attention back to the present. She smiled politely and turned back to the two at the table.

"My apologies, I have been rather sleepless," she said almost shyly. Servants had no doubt already spoken of her new lover. And by the glances exchanged between the two men, she knew they thought the same.

"No need to apologize, Your Majesty," Callus said before clearing his throat. As always, Dimitrius said nothing, his hands clasped on the table. Callus turned more fully towards her.

"We heard that Prince Castlier has expressed his desire to court you," he said, and for a moment she froze. Her hands fiddled with her skirt, but her face remained calm as she turned to Callus.

"The prince has, in a rather diplomatic letter," she said, and Dimitrius let out a scoff. When it came from Emris, she could find it amusing, but there was nothing funny about his tone.

"Your Highness, every matter concerning courtship is diplomatic," Dimitrius said.

For a moment, she sat there glaring at him.

"Are you mocking me?" she asked in an almost angry tone. He had always diminished her, not even addressing her on most occasions, but this-- this was just plain disrespect.

"No, Your Majesty, just stating a well-known fact. Courtships between kingdoms are rare and rarely center around genuine romance," he said, and even though it hit her like an arrow to the chest, she nodded.

Callus hummed in agreement.

"It is wonderful news indeed," Callus continued, his hands clasped on the table as well. There was no question whether she would court him. She knew they wanted her to. Dramira was a neighbouring kingdom that always provided generously for Cyneria.

She tried to speak, but Callus interjected once more.

"Dramira has such a large influx of precious materials, and with your union to the prince, it will bring even more prosperity. Their militia is advanced enough that we would be able to ward off a large invasion from the other side of the wall." He sounded as if he were trying to convince her of something she knew fully well.

Hours passed, and by the time she finally slipped out of the council room, her head was aching. In that moment, all her thoughts fled her when she realized she had not heard of Emris at all.

She felt her heart throbbing in her chest as she made her way to his room. She did not knock; she went inside. She found nothing and no one inside the room. He could not have gone to tell the advisors, could he? It was his word against hers. If it had all been to get close enough to take her crown-

Just then, she glanced at the balcony, and as she stepped out into the windy weather, she spotted him in the gardens.

She saw two things that would never fit together. Firstly, Emris curled up under the oak tree, which swayed with the wind. She could not imagine him outside, surrounded by bugs and heat. Secondly, he had a book in his hands.

Upon approaching him, she noticed the cat lounging in the tree above him, tail swishing in the wind as if they were suddenly close. He did not glance at her for a moment, and then he spoke.

"How was the meeting?"

"You read all of a sudden," she said, crossing her arms as she looked down at him. He glanced up at him. The dream flooded her mind at the sight of those eyes, the same shade filled with memories of the sea, feverish dreams she would not soon forget.

"I always read; you just never seem to catch me doing so since you are so busy trying to stab me." He said, flipping the page. She looked at him skeptically.

"Where did you get it?" "The palace library."

Her frustration flooded her. No one ever went into the library except her and a few servants who occasionally had time to skim the pages. The fact that he had invited himself there without asking made her angry.

"I didn't give you permission," she said, and then he closed the book and set it aside. His face looked tired, as if something had troubled him. She shoved away the urge to ask if something had happened.

"As your lover, I have as many privileges in the palace as you do," he said, and she scoffed. He was truly unbelievable. He stood, then, as she was already walking away; he came up beside her, his hand on the book as he followed closely after her.

"Shouldn't you be stealing bread from the kitchen?" She asked sarcastically, her hands fisted in her skirt to keep them out of the grass. The sun was high in the sky, and she did not care if the cat followed. She had not gotten close to it in a few hours, and if he could keep giving her dreams, the cat might decide to leave.

Emris chuckled.

"I'm not a pig, Valerie," he said, and she hated how her name on his lips made a shiver trace down her spine. For a moment, they just walked through the garden. She did not know what to speak of; she knew there was more to Morana than she knew, but something about his eyes made her avoid speaking of it.

"Where were you born?" She asked, and for a moment, he considered what she had asked.

A Cynerian accent, so his birthplace was probably farther.

"Closer to the wall, in Cyneria, of course," he said, and for a moment, she was surprised. He did not carry a Cynerian accent, so his birthplace being farther from the ocean made sense. Seeing him in a small home close to the wall, fell off.

142

She did not prod him with questions about his family, whether they knew he was a conduit, or whether they were still alive. It didn't matter, not really. She wasn't paying attention to her surroundings, and when one of the guards appeared in front of her, she nearly gasped.

"Your Majesty, I have a report from Linra."

She nodded, waiting, aware that Emris was still watching the interaction.

"We found sorcerers, Your Majesty." At the words, her gut clenched. The sorcerers had been quiet as of late, and she had hoped it would stay that way. For a moment, she just stood there and felt Emris watching her. He must have known her obligation. But for a moment, she wanted to challenge it. She stuffed it down for a moment and decided she would retire to her room. Emris did not bother following her.

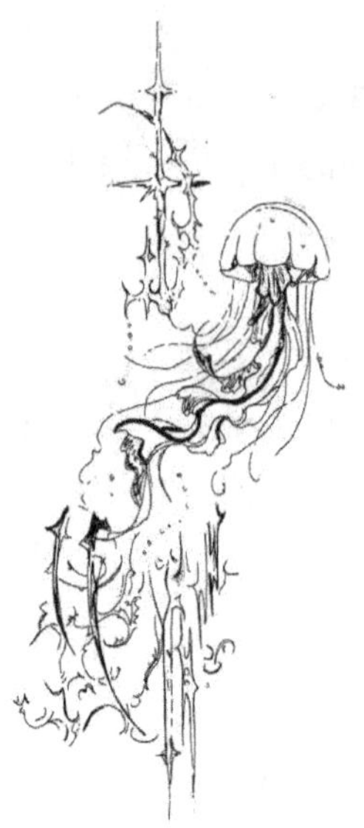

Chapter 23

That night, after dinner, she found herself sitting in her bedroom with Emris lounging by the chair. She needed to know more about Morana and what it meant to be a conduit. Emris had rolled up his sleeves, and he looked exhausted, but she dared not ask why.

Valerie sat on her bed, knees tucked to her chest. The cat lounged on the bed, and she pretended it wasn't there. The shadows had not bothered her since the dream with Morana, and she did not intend to entice them. He had brought a map to her room, and as she waited in silence, he laid it out on the floor as if to demonstrate something.

"What are you doing?" She asked with a small laugh, baffled at his strange way of explaining things.

"You'll see," he said, and after laying it out on the floor, he stood to his full height once more. She beheld the map, with the three human kingdoms side by side and the few oceanic islands. The other side of the wall was not well mapped, as if scribbled in haste. How much did they truly know about the different kingdoms?

"Emris?"

"Yes, sweetheart?"

She had stopped pretending the name didn't fluster her; she just schooled her features.

"Are there many conduits left?" She asked, and then he nodded. He took a moment to collect his thoughts.

"Are you familiar with all the gods?"

She shook her head. Her mother had never entertained her tutors who tried to teach her about the countless gods; they did not worship them, so, in her eyes, they were useless.

Besides, her mother had wanted nothing to do with the things responsible for allowing her husband to die.

"There are only a few gods who choose conduits. Now, I do not know all their names either, for I am not a priest. Ciro and Morana are two of them." He then pointed to the topmost kingdom on the other side of the wall.

Vescuria stood out to her in bold letters.

"There are a few scattered amongst the faerie lands," he said, swooping his hand downward to the tip of the farthest continent south. He did not stop, but his eyes lingered on some places more than others. Her curiosity got hold of her.

"Have you ever seen the faerie lands? Can conduits go see them?" she asked. She hated that she wanted to see the faerie lands, which she wanted to experience the beauty her mother had hated since her father's death.

Emris smiled softly before bringing the map over to the bed. He nestled it in the sheets before he spoke again.

"I have." He spoke softly, and she just watched him, waiting for him to continue.

Her heart was thudding loudly. He pointed to the topmost continent.

"Vecuria is beautiful, an oasis of sand and heat." As he spoke, she felt her heart pounding loudly in her ears; she had always wanted to know what lay behind the wall. His hand trailed down to the land just below it. He seemed to pause for a moment.

"Krovaria has many hills and green landscapes, and it is always warm like summer." He smiled softly as if remembering his time spent there. For a moment, her chest twinged with a longing to see the kingdom. His hand moved down to the next.

"Liseria is a more barren land filled with emptiness; it is quite lonely there," he said almost sorrowfully, but she couldn't help gazing at it as if it were the heavens. His hand swept down once more to the kingdom at the bottom tip of the continent.

"Saelia is much like Cyneria. It is built on the ocean and is very beautiful."

Her heart felt as if it might leap out of her chest. Her mother had told her to fear the faeries, to run from them. And yet, here it seemed as if she could see the faerie lands, experience the beauty that Emris had merely scathed. She turned to find he was watching her with an almost observant gaze, and she blinked.

"How did you see them all?" she asked in wonderment. It was rare for humans to travel to the Faerie lands. Furthermore, if they somehow scaled the wall or got through the gate, they were often killed on the other side. He stepped back from the bed, his hand running over his face. She realized he must be exhausted.

"When I was a boy, Ciro chose me," he said, as if remembering a dream.

His eyes met hers, and he sat down on the edge of the bed, carefully discarding the map on the floor.

Her nerves fluttered, but she didn't take her eyes off him.

"I did not know what I had become until my father was killed. I spent months trying to understand why your-" His voice stopped, as if afraid to mention her dead mother.

She just shook her head and then nodded for him to continue.

"She had my father executed in front of my eyes. I was only eight. She had been asking if he knew of any sorcerers in the area. He had denied it until his deathbed, protecting me." She had the urge to reach over and touch him, to apologize for her mother's sins. But she knew she was no better.

"Afterwards, Ciro led me to the other side of the wall. I still can't understand how or why, but I found myself wandering the faerie lands before I was twelve.

He said, examining his hands, almost sadly, his brow had creased.

She felt the guilt gnawing at her, slowly eating away at her.

Then he turned.

"I heard about your father, I'm sorry," he said softly. She tensed. No one spoke of her father's death, as if her coronation, timed with her mother's untimely death, had pulled the people away from her father's memory. She focused on the sheets beneath her. If she let herself, she would start to cry. But she would not cry in front of him.

"As am I," she whispered. The cat made its way to her. Its presence around the castle was ever constant, and for a moment, she tensed. Emris watched her as she gently petted the cat's head, and it purred into her hand.

"Sometimes it's easy to forget that Morana is always watching," she said softly as if speaking to herself. Emris was watching as her eyes latched onto her face. He nodded as if in understanding. They were much more alike than she knew. She tried not to wince as the cat purred into her hand once more. She was still watching her as she turned to look at him, and a small smile broke out on her face at his expression.

"What?" she asked in her soft voice. Emris looked as if he had stopped breathing; his breath hitched visibly.

"I've never heard you laugh before," he said, as if in shock.

She flushed red.

"I know it sounds hor-"

"Do it again," he said, his eyes locking on her face.

She looked at him, her brow cocked.

"You don't think it sounds too strained, or…?"

He shook his head at the question, his eyes tracing her face, and, for a moment, the purring cat disappeared.

It was just the two of them.

"We shouldn't be laughing," she said softly, reminded once more that Morana could do something horrid any second. But then she felt him shift, before she knew what was happening, he was sitting so close she was sure he could hear her thundering heartbeat. The cat had moved toward the chair.

"Never apologize for a sound so beautiful," he said, and her heart thundered, her face flushed.

"You're not afraid of me, are you?" She asked hesitantly. Morana had a grip on her, no doubt; she would soon feel it. She would become whatever mould the goddess pushed her into. But somehow, what he thought mattered.

"Quite the opposite, actually," he said, and she met his eyes, licked her lips. His eyes caught the motion.

"And what is the opposite of fear?" She asked, her hands clenching in her lap hard enough that her knuckles were nearly white.

"Reverence," he breathed, and she stopped thinking for a moment.

She felt the urge to reach for him, to thread her fingers through his hair and bring her lips to his.

Still, she resisted.

Emris watched her with so much emotion that she couldn't take her eyes off him.

Morana's leash would run out soon enough, and then what? She would become whatever she wanted. Her kingdom was plundered. Her executed. For a moment, her mind blanked. She wanted one thing, and for a moment it frightened her.

"If I ask you for a favour, would you do it?" She asked him, her voice serious now, even as her face paled; she could not breathe, she could not think.

"Anything," he breathed, and for a moment she looked up.

Upon seeing her face, his brow creased in confusion.

"When Morana takes over me, when I can't fight for myself, I need you to…"

She closed her eyes to stop herself from shaking.

"I need you to kill me," she whispered, barely audibly.

The words hung in the air like a noose. For a moment, no one seemed to breathe. She needed someone who was not loyal to her throne to do it. Seraphina would never do it; she would rather die in his hands than be corrupted by Morana to the point of madness.

She met his eyes then; a deep sorrow flitted over his face, and for a moment, he seemed to focus on her as if admiring a muse.

"You ask for too much," he whispered, and she was shocked. She stared at him before standing; she could not meet his gaze. How could he suggest she keep living if Morana completely controlled her?

"Valerie, you must under-" He suddenly hesitated. He, reaching out to touch her bare arm,

She flinched as if struck. She was back on that balcony again.

She spun around, tears burning her eyes.

"No, Emris, *you* must understand. She will take over my mind; you know it as well as I do. I am prepared to die to save my kingdom from her. I am prepared to give up everything I have ever known, and yet you deny me that right,"

She was yelling now, tears burning her eyes.

"You have no idea what it is to live with a monster inside your head. You have no idea how much I loathe looking into that cursed mirror, in case she shows her terrifying head. I do not sleep, and I eat only so I do not starve." She was furious, her heart pounding. Tears blurred her vision, and she stumbled back, dropping her head into her hands, palms pressed to her eyes. She met his gaze, and upon seeing her, he flinched as if struck. He did not approach her, but the pain in his eyes spoke enough.

"I believed you cared," she scoffed. "My mother was right," she said, her voice breaking on the word mother.

"I am a fool," she whispered, her hands shaking. She could not think straight; all her grief overwhelmed her, and for a moment, she just stood there watching him as if he had betrayed her.

He stood then, and she took a step back.

"Don't look at me as if I am nothing but a monster on the verge of unspeakable evil, Emris. Don't try to convince me that I am still myself. You will lose me, too," she said, and he swallowed thickly.

She watched as his throat bobbed and his eyes flicked over her.

He opened his mouth to speak, but pain shot through her again; this time it built behind her eyes like a crescendo. Her hands started to shake, and she realized the cat was gone; the candles that had been lit were extinguished.

Emris froze where he was, not daring to step closer.

The shadows curled around her wrists and hands like chains. Her throat bobbed, and she tried to stop herself from sobbing, but she could not.

"Emris," she choked out, as if in pain.

Before she could understand what was happening, arms came around her. He was shaking, the shadows curled around him, too, and he looked as if he were being burned.

"No, Emris, you'll-"

He just held onto her like she was a lifeline.

She was pressed to his chest, even as she tried to push away. He grunted, and she shoved at his chest again, but he did not let go. Her hands shook, and she couldn't breathe.

Then that voice purred in her head again.

Such a noble boy. Shame.

She felt his arms loosen around her as shadows enwrapped him. Her scream was muffled as he collapsed in front of her, and she dropped to her knees.

Chapter 24

When darkness dragged her under this time, she was not afraid. She was furious.

She stumbled in the dark.

"Morana!"

She screamed repeatedly. Had she killed him? The thought made her feel sick. She kept screaming for Morana, desperate to beg for his life if needed be.

In the distance, she saw the goddess sitting on her throne. Before Valerie could stop herself, she was hurtling towards her. The woman seemed preoccupied, looking at her long nails. Valerie was panting when she reached her.

"Where is he?" She demanded, and her hands were shaking. Morana shifted her eyes away from her to look past her.

"Did you seriously believe I would kill him? No sweet thing, I would not dare aggravate Ciro," she said sarcastically.

Valerie spun around and there, suddenly…

Emris stood there, glowing gold, a shade lighter than his eyes, gold lines covering his body, and he wore nothing but a pair of trousers as if his shirt had been ripped from him.

She was running towards him faster than she had ever run before. She reached out to grab his hand but slammed into the barricade. She fell backwards, hitting the ground hard.

"What did you do to him?" She yelled at Morana. The goddess could strike her down if she wished to. She did not move from her throne.

"I did nothing to him, Valerie, except show you exactly what he is," Morana said, and Valerie whirled again, looking at Emris through the barricade, his face still visible; he wasn't looking at her, just standing there.

"I know he is a conduit," she demanded, anger flaring, and before she could move, Morana was behind her. She did not snap at her for raising her voice; instead, she placed her hands firmly on her shoulders and urged her to look closer.

"Can he hear us?" She asked, her throat bobbing, and she pressed her hand to the barricade as if touching him.

"No."

"I don't understand. I knew he was a conduit," Valerie said, but Morana's nails dug into her skin slightly, urging her to take a closer look. She observed him carefully and watched as his rounded ears turned pointed, as if a veil had slipped off him.

She had seen them on so many sorcerers that she stumbled back. Morana missed her, and she landed hard.

"It's not possible," she gasped out, trying to close her eyes, but she couldn't. Emris was not just a conduit.

He was a faerie.

Valerie felt as if an arrow had struck her straight through the chest; betrayal tasted sour in her mouth as she beheld him in his proper form. His jawline sharper, eyes glowing more brightly, the markings on his chest etched in a language she could not comprehend. Morana said nothing but lingered nearby.

She finally understood how he knew so much about the other kingdoms across the wall; he was from them. She moved away from the barricade. She could not stop the fear that coursed through her. Faeries were stronger, smarter, and much more deadly than humans.

"How could I have been so stupid?" she whispered,

Morana drew near, her eyes almost soft, if that was even possible.

"Ciro cast an illusion over his features; you could not have known." Morana seemed to understand the feeling of betrayal.

"You cannot tell him you know; he will kill you."

She felt her heart thud loudly in her chest as if it might burst; she nodded silently. Her eyes burned with tears. She had thought Morana would be the monster, but now it appeared that Emris had taken the title.

"If you call to the shadows, they will answer to you," Morana whispered softly and then tucked one of her curls behind her ear. Valerie was struck by how suddenly Morana had succumbed to leniency. Was she plotting?

Morana whispered a single word.

"Wake."

Valerie's eyes snapped open. Emris lay on the ground before her; he stirred. She felt her whole chest constrict. He was a faerie, and he hadn't told her. She knew she could not demand the truth from him, and yet it burned to know he wouldn't tell her. She forced herself to remain calm as she beheld him; she met his eyes as he sat up.

"Are you hurt?" He demanded sitting forward as if to reach for her, and she resisted the urge to flinch. Valerie knew if she told him she knew what he was, he would kill her.

"No," she said softly, then looked at him, really looked at him. Maybe if he saw the need in her eyes, he would tell her. But she saw nothing in his eyes. Ciro was good at creating a believable guise; she could not see the points of his ears or the higher cheekbones. Before he could say anything, she made her way to her bed.

"I am sorry for what happened," she said. She could not forget the fear that had coursed through her, could not explain that in those moments she thought he was dead, something inside her chest had cracked.

Emris did not respond; he watched her eyes, softer than she had ever seen them.

Then they hardened in an instant.

"Good night," he said and made his way to the door. She wanted to call after him, demand why he had lied to her, why he had been deceiving her this whole time. But she didn't.

She had believed his lies, that he only wanted to speak to Morana. But if he could lie about his identity, what else could he be lying about?

The door shut behind him, and for a moment she sat there under the covers, her heart beating with throbs of pain. She could not believe that she had thought for one moment that he truly cared for her.

Her eyes fluttered shut, and for once, she did not fear Morana calling her name.

Chapter 25

Emris made his way to his room. He knew something was wrong. He had been dragged under by Morana but had not awoken again in the realm. His hands clenched into fists at his side as soon as he stepped into his room.

Ciro had said so little about what he was meant to do here. It felt as if he was wasting time.

His heart ached, nonetheless.

He had wrapped his arms around her even though he had remembered Morana's threat to kill him. It didn't matter at that moment; none of it did. Emris sat down on the bed; his hands folded in front of him.

You are a fool.

Ciro snapped in his head; he already had an ache, and the gods yelling did not help with it.

"Why exactly?"

Ciro let out a dry, unamused laugh at his sarcasm.

You let Morana get a hold of you.

Ciro barked in his head, and Emris' head snapped up.

"That's impossible, I wasn't in the realm," he said, standing now, jaw clenched tightly. "What did she do?"

I could not get through to her; the barricade was too strong, and I could not see past it.

Emris swore under his breath. He could not understand why Valerie had looked at him that way, like there was something horribly wrong.

"Did the guise drop?" Emris asked, his voice now shaking. Ciro had assured him the guise would hold firm, that he could be among the humans without being spotted. But against Morana, nothing was certain.

He found his heart racing. If the guise had dropped and Valerie saw-

No.

He let out a breath he didn't know he was holding. He dropped his head into his hands, breathing deeply. He had felt the darkness take him, but-

She had been worth every inch of pain he had experienced. And that frightened him.

"When do you want to speak with Morana?" he asked, noting that he would have to get inside the barricade, and for that to happen, Valerie would have to let him in.

Soon, Ciro murmured inside his head.

Emris lost another breath before lying down on his bed. Ciro had been more distant as of late. Before he had ventured into Cyneria, the god had been a constant presence in his head; now he was nothing more than a whisper.

Had Morana scared him?

Morana was the most dangerous of all the gods. Closest only to Vazeer, who was as unpredictable as his conduit. Morana could kill Ciro if she got her hands on him; she could kill any of the gods-

And yet she kept Valerie alive. He ran a hand through his hair again. Emris did not know what Ciro wanted to say to Morana. All he knew was that questioning Ciro was not something he had any interest in doing. His patience was waning thin. He seemed even more disgruntled than he had been months before. Something was going on, something that Ciro would not tell Emris. And although Emris knew gods were mysterious and would do what they pleased, the thought of Ciro hiding something from him sent his blood chilling.

Especially if it was something about Valerie.

Chapter 26

The next morning, Valerie could not focus on the advisors around the table. Her mind was in a far-off place, where Emris was a faerie, a place where he was hiding it from her.

But why?

She had spent all night racking her mind for the reason why he would do it. She did not have the right to demand any answers from him. He was a faerie conduit, and in her land it spelled death. She had summoned the advisors to speak to them about something that could not be avoided any longer. Sorcerers.

Callus sat at his seat, playing with a pen, while Arminia, back from her tour of the border, sat stonily in her chair, her face paler than usual. Dimitrius stared at the table as if it were a pond. All her advisors looked exhausted. She did not blame them.

Since she had encountered Emris that night, everything else had been forgotten temporarily. She knew she had to be careful. One wrong movement, one outburst from Morana, and it would all go to hell. Callus spoke first as if annoyed with the silence.

"I have been informed that you have not dealt with two sorcerers," he said, and for a moment, Valerie held her breath. She had forgotten about them; there had been more important things to address. Emris flashed in her mind, his eyes scanning her face, telling her he would come for her. She blinked before raising her head slightly.

"We are all aware that my mother had a strict way of making sure faeries and sorcerers stayed outside of our lands." She swallowed back the grief that she had still not processed.

"I do not intend to be my mother," she said, and for a moment, all the advisors froze. Her mother had been slaughtering sorcerers and faeries for the past ten years. Valerie clenched her fists in her skirts. If she wanted to survive, she would need to amend the law.

"Are you proposing we stop executing them?" Dimitrius asked, his voice laced with something akin to anger. She was shocked to see them all staring at her, brows creased, frowns heavy on their faces.

"Yes," she said. That one word could kill her or save her.

The three advisors did not speak for a moment, then Arminia's voice cut through the air, icy and cold.

"If we abolish that law, we are dooming ourselves to another war," she said. Arminia had been her mother's dearest friend, had seen the madness that had taken over her mother at the behest of murdering sorcerers. How could she accept the murder of innocent people?

"We cannot continue to butcher a people who are innocent," Valerie replied, and then Callus stood from his chair, his hands clenched into fists on the table, his brow creased.

"What you are proposing is a genocide of our people," he said loudly, and Valerie almost flinched. She could feel Morana scraping her nails against her mental barricade, one that would no doubt erupt if she did not get this meeting under control.

"If we stop killing them now, we are dooming ourselves. There could be spies sent to infiltrate our camps, our towns-" Callus broke off as Arminia nodded.

"Your mother might not have been a queen of finery, but she was a queen of war, and her system has ensured that our people remain safe."

Valerie felt the rejection boiling in her gut. She could not understand how her own advisors could endorse her murdering innocents purely for magic.

She stood, anger flaring in her chest, Morana clawed at her chest, and she forced herself to remain calm.

"If you want to continue this cycle, I will not stop you, since you are both so adamant in assuming that murdering innocents will continue to protect our lands." Callus opened his mouth to speak, but she merely raised a hand to stop him.

"But I will not be a murderer," she said simply, and all the advisors looked at each other for a moment before looking back at Valerie.

"Arminia, you will oversee executions if that is what you believe will protect our lands."

She turned to the woman and met her eyes; she could not stop the fear curdling in her gut. If any of them suspected she was a conduit or even a sorcerer, she would be put under the same noose. Arminia nodded before Valerie slipped out of the room. She reached her room within minutes.

The cat sprawled on the bed and did not move as she made her way to the bathing room and retched into the basin. Did murdering sorcerers and faeries truly protect her people? Or was it just an incarnation of her mother's rage?

Valerie sagged against the basin.

If it were true, she could not jeopardize her people, yet she knew that continuing to murder innocents would come to haunt her. Valerie knew then that she was playing the fool. Even though sorcerers would continue to be murdered outside the walls, she was keeping someone safe who could upturn her kingdom and drag her down with him.

That night, she did not go down to dinner. She could not look at Emris without feeling betrayed. She could not risk her mind being laid bare to him. Valerie rarely visited the palace library.

When she was a child, her father would whisk her away to the space, spend hours showing her maps or telling extravagant stories. That was before the war, before he had fought and come back changed. She could not remember much of him when he came back. He had been distant, hollow in a sense. Then two years later, he died. Valerie had not set foot inside the library since her mother died. The two brown doors swung open, and for a moment, she stood there.

Thousands of books sat in neat rows on hundreds of shelves around the room. The walls were lined with shelves and ladders, and servants waded through stacks of books to neatly arrange the archives. Scrolls were kept in small cabinets on one of the lower walls, and the spiral staircase led down into the lower section of the library. Her feet seemed to tread on memories as she slowly made her way deeper into the space. Once it had been a refuge, before tutors and maps and royalty, before the crown was thrust upon her as a child. Expectations burned away her childhood like a flame to kindling.

Her hands were slightly clenched as she made her way deeper into the space. Candles were lit and scattered throughout the space to further illuminate it. She had come there knowing she was looking for answers that were impossible to find.

She wandered the space until she reached the section archived for gods. The human kingdoms did not worship them, but they kept scrolls and books by priestesses as if to preserve the knowledge in case another conduit rose.

As far as Valerie knew, she was the first ever conduit in Cyneria. And would no doubt be the last. She had not let herself think about how her life would be led. How could she possibly sustain the crown?

Her hands traced the spines of the books, each of them thick and worn with age. Since her mother's crowning, very few priestesses had deemed it to record their visions. Her mother had never told her the prophecy made for her reign.

Every royal in Cyneria was given one upon accepting the crown.

A shiver traced down her spine. She had the urge to ask Morana for wisdom, but she doubted Morana would want that door open. She was not sure she could close it. But she steeled herself enough to enter that space inside her mind. Morana had promised the shadows would answer her if she called them. She turned to make sure no one was nearby, then reached into her mind once more. She did not need to speak to summon them; they came willingly.

She needed answers about Emris, needed to know the full extent of Morana's power. The shadows, as if sensing her curiosity, appeared in the form of the cat. She nearly jumped. She had not remembered the cat following her. Its green eyes met hers before it made its way to one of the shelves. Carefully, it rubbed against one of the books and then moved aside. Valerie's hands shook slightly as she reached for the tome. It was heavy in her arms, and she barely managed to put it down on the ground before she sat down beside it. No one could know what she was doing.

She opened the book as quietly as she could, stopping it before it thudded to the ground. The cat curled up beside her, its tail curling over her ankle, and she did not flinch from its touch. Her hands trembled slightly as she began to flip through the old pages. Her eyes scanned the writing, scribbled in pitch-black ink.

Her eyes landed on a particular page, her heart thundering. Something drew her to it, and she found herself reading it in her head:

These words have been recorded by the Priestess of the gods under the reign of King Judas.

I have wandered the faerie lands with my king. I cannot begin to describe the horrors of these foreign people. They are not like us, and they do not think like us. We have no way to defeat them should a war descend upon us. All we can do is pray.

The words sent a shiver down her spine. She flipped the page, seeking more information, but found none. In all her years, she had never truly learned much about the faerie people; she knew little, even from the spies her mother had spoken with.

Even now, there was no one she could trust to find information for her.

She closed the book and stood, sliding it back onto the shelf. The cat was still sitting when she stood. As she walked through the library, she spotted different servants wearing dark black garb.

Assassins and spies were not uncommon in Cyneria. They had been indebted to her mother, and now they were indebted to her. Valerie assumed Arminia had tasked them with killing the sorcerers now that Valerie herself refused to do it.

Her hands were shaking by the time she opened the doors to the garden. The cat followed her, trailing leisurely beside her as Emris had done days earlier. She clenched her hands tightly as the night air hit her face and the stars shone brightly above the now-dark garden. Lamps illuminated the pathways branching into the green brush. Guards were stationed closer to the palace, and no one followed her. She doubted she needed protection at all.

Morana was a goddess of jealousy, and anyone who laid a hand on her would die within seconds. She couldn't stop her eyes from blinking back tears as fear coursed through her. She watched as Emris dropped to the ground in front of her, and for a moment she thought he was dead, that she had killed him.

A part of her couldn't make peace with the thought of murdering innocents. Valerie did not know if Emris was innocent. He had lied to her about his identity; he could no doubt lie to her about his true intentions. Her hands reached out to grasp hold of a rose, but instead, she watched as shadows became an extension of her fingers. She gasped, pulling her hand back into her sleeve.

For a moment, she debated returning to the palace, forgetting the way the shadows had done what she pleased. But running from power was what would get her killed.

Slowly, her hand reached back out into the night air, and the shadows curled around the rose. She feared she would strangle the life out of the flower, but instead, the shadows merely grasped it weakly.

She felt fear in her chest.

Emris had not taught her anything; he had merely spoken of what would happen. How did he know? She pulled her hand back, and the shadows retreated. She found herself whispering something to the shadows. If what Morana had promised held true, he would get more answers than he would tell her directly.

Without another moment, the shadows curled away from her and followed the path she had set.

She felt like a weight was pressing down on her shoulders as the shadows slid into Emris' room.

Chapter 27

Emris hadn't stayed at the dinner table long. When he realized Valerie would not be joining any time soon, he left the dining hall. He made his way back to his room, hands stuffed into his pockets. His head throbbed with a migraine.

The balcony door was open as he had left it.

The candles were still burning, and the sound of the ocean crashing in the distance reached him as he made his way to the small closet. He stripped off his shirt, revealing his scarred torso in the mirror a few feet away. The golden skin was covered in deep gashes, and the muscles were clearly visible. His trousers came off next, leaving him bare. He made his way to the bathing chambers.

He took a few minutes to fill the bathtub. While he waited, he turned to the mirror above the sink; his body had remained strong in the few weeks since his departure from Krovaria. He hadn't been able to continue sparring or training, yet his physique hadn't changed in the slightest. He sighed, letting his head fall back, white hair grazing the back of his shoulders.

After a few minutes of the water pouring into the circular bath, he climbed in. He groaned low at the feeling of the warm water engulfing him. He was still at first, then he moved to grab a bar of white soap, starting to lather it before scrubbing his chest.

He sat there after washing himself, staring at the wall, his hands twitching on the rims of the bath, a muscle flexing in his jaw. Something was wrong, he knew. Valerie seemed off.

After a few more minutes of soaking, he lifted himself out of the water. The cold hit him, and he shivered involuntarily, the water dripping off his body onto the floor, before he grasped a towel to start drying himself off.

After draining the water and combing a hand through his hair, he wrapped the towel around his waist and made his way to the bed. He slipped into a pair of sleep trousers before sitting on the edge of the bed. Emris tried to convince himself that sleep would find him, but he knew it wouldn't.

Instinctively, he reached for the dagger he kept tucked under his pillow. The guise shielded him from other mortals' sight. He was much taller in that form, more toned, stronger, with longer canines and pointed ears that would give him away instantly. He sighed, running his tongue over his duller canines. He gripped the small whetstone he had packed and rubbed it against the blade. The sound of the blade sharpening filled the room.

He almost didn't notice it when the shadows shifted. If it had not been for the utter quiet, suddenly, he would not have turned his attention upwards and caught a glimpse of the wisps tracking him across the floor. The wind blew as the shadows crept silently through the room.

Emris smirked. He did not know if this was Morana's or Valerie's doing. Ciro had been slow to act last time. Emris knew his god would not make the same mistake again.

Slowly, he stood and acknowledged the shadows, as if acknowledging an adversary. Ciro had warned him that Morana would bring shadows after him at some point. He walked slowly out into the center of the room and did not cower as the shadows slowly slid towards him, not hiding, knowing it was foolish. With a flick of his wrist, he let the dagger fall to the bed, hitting the linens with a soft thud. For a moment, he let his head tip back, throat bare to the ceiling as he sighed.

If this were Valerie's doing, he would have to admit she was becoming sly.

With a flick of his wrist, light flickered over his skin in wisps of gold. The shadows did not pause even as the wisps of his own light illuminated the room. They glided over his bare chest, down his arms, until they slithered over his feet. The shadows seemed to pause at the sight, then they transformed before his eyes.

He did not retreat as the panther slowly approached him, licking its white teeth, tall, dragging leisurely behind it. The animal had those green eyes that the cat had always possessed.

Emris smirked, not in the least bit startled. If Morana wanted to kill him, she could, and yet the animal did not pounce. It curled around his ankle, muscles shifting against his calf.

Emris let his hand drop down to the cat's view. The cat nudged its hand with its head, purring low in its throat as its sleek black fur rubbed against its hand.

The cat vanished, fading as if they had never been there. Emris knew that Valerie had sent the shadows. He did not know why, but she had spared him. If she wanted him dead, the panther would have killed him. As his magic vanished from his hand, he found himself smirking softly.

And for a moment, he found himself questioning if the Cynerian queen hated him as much as she let on.

Chapter 28

The next morning, Valerie made her way down to breakfast. She knew that avoiding Emris was futile. The shadows had whispered nothing, and the small house cat curled at her feet on the bed. Her chest tightened as she finally made her way to the dining hall.

He sat there, and she found her hands clenching. He did not look up at her immediately; instead, he sipped his juice. She was supposed to play his lover; he was supposed to play the role. He looked the part, no doubt.

Valerie knew they had to maintain their facade; if it fell away, he might risk being seen for what he truly was.

She reached the table, and his eyes lifted. She had expected anger and resentment in his eyes, but there was a slight hint of amusement in those golden eyes as she finally sat down beside him. The servants, upon seeing her enter the room, began bringing food to the table— eggs, freshly scrambled with parsley, and sweet tarts made with strawberries.

Valerie felt her mind spinning, her hands clenched in her lap. The betrayal still burned in her chest. She could not look at him. Then, without her noticing, he slipped closer, and she found herself frozen as his breath tickled her neck.

"I enjoyed your gift," he purred, and she tensed, her heart rate spiked. Could he hear it beating under her skin? She knew he could.

"I do not know what you are referring to," she whispered back at him quietly. She nodded politely as a servant poured her some juice, and she turned, finding his eyes latching onto her face. She felt like a sheep under the gaze of a wolf. He was a faerie, and she knew so little about his kind.

Emris chuckled slightly as he sat back. He started to eat quietly, and she found her eyes looking over him again as if to catch a crack in his guise. If she had not seen his proper form in the realm, she would not have ever believed he was a faerie. He chewed on his apple slice and then swallowed.

"Have you always made it a habit of yours to stare at me?" He asked without looking at her, heat shot to her face traitorously. Her eyes glanced to the windows overlooking the ocean. She missed the caves, the quiet that they brought.

"Have you made it a habit to pester me with nonsense constantly?" she quipped, turning to find him watching her. She smiled in a way that cut through bone. His eyes flicked to her mouth, and she resisted the urge to lick her lips.

"Is that really how you speak to your lover?" He asked, running a finger over the rim of his glass; heat flared low in her stomach. He had said it loud enough that all the guards around the room could hear. It guaranteed her safety for a few more days.

"Is that really how you speak to your queen?" She replied, and he scoffed a soft laugh.

"What makes you think you are my queen?" He asked in a voice, teetering on annoyance, she could not tell if it was forced.

"Are you asking me or telling me?" She sipped her juice again, her eyes never leaving his.

"I would expect you to be my lover, not my court advisor," she said

He smirked before saying, just loud enough to send a shiver down her spine.

"I would be whatever you asked of me, your majesty. Fool, knight, priest. I would be a god if you merely asked me."

Her hand tightened in her skirt. He always had a way of saying things that made her heart flutter. She found her mouth slightly dry, so she took a bite of the eggs. Her white dress with a leather corset was different from her usual attire, but it still squeezed her ribs.

She took a bite of the strawberry pastry and nearly moaned. The palace baker really did have a way of making her pastries taste like paradise. She swallowed and froze. Emris had leaned forward ever so slightly, and she could feel the heat of his body on her chest. He reached over his hand and ever so gently wiped a stray bit of jam off her lower lip. Her breath hitched as he brought his thumb to his own lips.

"Sweet," he said, sitting back, his eyes never leaving hers.

Her face was flushed, and she felt heat flare in her chest. She tried to convince herself that she had to be wary, that she had to fear him. And yet those golden eyes made everything else seem like a feverish dream.

She found heat flaring so violently in her chest that she pushed back from the table.

"Excuse me," she said softly, and his eyes immediately flicked to her. She found hatred flaring at how easily he disarmed her defences.

Faeries were beautiful creatures who preyed on the weak. She would not be weak. Without another word, she made her way to her room, cursing at the heat in her face and the hint of wanting in her gut.

For the first time in a while, Valerie found herself sitting at her desk. She hadn't touched it since that night weeks ago, when General Ladib had been executed. She folded herself onto the desk, her arms making a soft pillow for her head. She felt as if she had been punched in the gut. Between trying to keep her kingdom going with constant

With bickering among her advisors, the threat of war, and the need to keep Morana's true identity secret, she found it hard to exist. She barely registered the knock on the door. It opened, and Seraphina stepped inside. Her friend looked at Valerie, hunched over her desk.

"Not getting much sleep, I am guessing?" Seraphina asked, and Valerie sat up, cheeks a bright red. She had to lie to her, so she nodded. In her friend's hand was an envelope, and for a moment she dreaded what it might contain.

Seraphina made her way to the desk and put it down on the surface. She recognized the script in an instant.

"The prince sends his regards," Seraphina said before moving to stand by the chair. She noticed the cat and moved to pet its head softly. Without giving herself time to hesitate, she tore open the white envelope, the seal slipping away.

"We were surveying the border of Dramira when one of his messengers told us to give this to you."

She barely heard Seraphina's words as her eyes scanned the page with dread. The words blurred by, and she clutched the paper. Seraphina stood there, hands folded, watching Valerie's face. After reading the letter, she placed it on the desk, her hands white from clenching.

"He is on his way to Cyneria; he will be here in two days."

After dinner that night, Valerie sat in tense silence. Valerie followed Emris out of the dining hall. He kept walking as if she weren't in desperate need of speaking with him. The prince's arrival would change everything, especially since he wanted to court her.

She finally caught up to him near his room, and she cleared her throat.

"We need to talk," she said, and he froze, turning slowly, his eyes latched onto her face, noting the tense set of her mouth.

"Of what?" He asked, continuing to walk towards his room. She could barely stop herself from running. He opened the door, and she followed, shutting it behind her. Being alone with him made her stomach clench. She waited for him to explain himself. But found nothing in his gaze.

"The prince will be here in two days to court me," she said. For a moment, he said nothing, then sighed, pinching the bridge of his nose with his index finger and thumb.

"And this should be spoken of, why?" he asked, and she had the urge to slap him across the face.

How could he speak with so little care?

She walked until she stood inches from him.

"When he arrives, he will no doubt question who you are," she said, her voice seething with anger.

"Tell him I am your lover; many queens have lovers in their marriages." She looked at him for a moment, then he turned, and she could see the cold look in his eyes.

"You expect me to marry him?" she said, almost angrily.

He let out a chuckle, showing he was anything but amused.

"I expect you to become his queen," he said, and she flinched as if struck. He did not even try to woo her out of it. She did not cower under his gaze; she could not cower before anyone else.

"Of course you would," she snapped at him, and he bristled slightly, his eyes meeting hers. He took a step forward. She hated how he doubted she could rule on her own—his queen. The words hit her deep in the chest.

She tried not to flinch as she met his eyes, anger filling her chest.

She wanted to hit him.

Hard.

"You seem angry," he said, now closer, and she whirled to him.

"Of course I am angry," she bit out. "You have no faith in my reign. You have no faith in me at all," she screamed at him.

He did not flinch.

She felt foolish; was she implying she wanted his validation?

She moved away from him.

"Is that really what you think, Valerie?" He asked, and she realized once more how beautiful her name sounded from his lips. She felt a flush creep on her cheeks, her brows still furrowed. He stepped closer, reaching for her, but she moved back slightly.

"You do not need my opinion, you could wear a crown, and I would gladly bow at your feet," he said, and for a moment she found it hard to know if he was speaking the truth. He was a faerie; the idea of him kneeling at her sounded foolish.

"Do you seriously believe I would have chased you into the realm, slammed my body against that barricade if I had no faith in you?" he asked, almost hurt. She met his eyes; those golden orbs stared into her very soul.

"Believe me, Valerie, I do not want you to marry him." She stood there for a moment, heart pounding in her chest; she bit her bottom lip slightly, and he caught the gesture.

"Then what do you want for me?"

His eyes fixed on her mouth, then flicked back up to her brown eyes. She felt as if the world narrowed in on them.

"If I told you, you would not believe me," he said with a small smile, and her gut twisted. She stood there, waiting.

"I do not want you to marry him or even consider courting him. But I know it is a foolish thing to ask of you." He stepped closer, gently tucking a curl behind her ear, and her eyes met his, no longer afraid at all.

"Why?"

"Your mind might always belong to Morana. I cannot change that. I am no worthy suitor or prince, and I know he will give you everything you desire. But I want to be the only one you give your heart to. For I shall guard it with my life."

The words hung in the air between them, and she felt her heart thud loudly in her chest. Valerie had the urge to reach for his hand. But she merely met his eyes. How could he mean that? After deceiving her…

"Forgive my foolishness."

She swallowed the words; his eyes dropped to the ground for a moment. He started to walk away, but she felt her conscience leave her as she grasped his wrist. Her hand barely held his whole wrist, and he froze. Slowly, he turned back to her.

"How can you say such things and then walk away from me?" she asked, dropping his hand. He turned to face her fully. His hand rose, and his index finger traced her jaw. She stopped breathing.

"Because if I stayed any longer, I would do something we would both regret." He whispered, and a shiver rolled down her spine. He pulled back his hand, retreating to his pocket.

She flinched at the loss, her heart in her throat. He watched her for a moment.

"What is it that you want?" He asked softly, and for a moment, she assumed she had misheard him.

"To take care of my peo-" "No, what do *you* want?"

No one had ever asked her what her heart desired, what she would have done with her life had the crown never been passed down to her. She stood there for a moment, cautious not to give her heart to him freely. For a moment, she thought about what he would say to her foolish dreams.

"To see the world, beyond the palace," she said. His eyes latched onto her face. She had never uttered her wantings, never spoken of them to another living soul, and yet saying it aloud did not fill her with shame. He did not judge her.

Valerie knew now that her dream was foolish. With her title, the threats of war, and the proposal to be courted. She knew that wanting anything other than her throne was foolish.

"I never told anyone that," she whispered, wringing her hands together like a towel. He did not laugh at her or smile; he looked at her, his eyes softened.

"Why not?"

"Because no one wants to hear a woman's dreams." She said it was the bitter truth. Men always found a way to undermine a woman's wants. To her people, she was nothing but a monarch, not a woman with dreams, dreams that could never be fulfilled.

Emris took a careful step towards her. He reached for her hand, and she did not flinch as his larger hand cupped hers. He lifted her hand to his mouth, and his lips grazed her knuckles. His eyes never left hers.

"I would spend days beside your bed to hear every single one of them. And if you let me, I will make every single one of them come true."

He slowly let go of her hand and smiled softly before slipping out of the room. For a moment, everything she knew about Emris, his real identity, his power, and his god, none of it mattered.

All that she knew for sure was that when Prince Castiler came to ask her to court, she might not say yes.

Chapter 29

The following two days passed in a blur, with teetering servants eager to know how to decorate the palace and prepare everything. Priestesses were brought to the palace to bless their courting should she accept his proposal.

Valerie tried to avoid thinking of Emris, his stupid smirk, and the way he had kissed her knuckles softly, as if she were something holy. Her advisors had spoken little of the union, other than that it would protect both nations should the foreign lands decide to launch an attack. What they were suggesting was the merging of two mighty bloodlines.

She sat in her room trying to breathe easily, but her mind was full of horrible things. She knew her advisors were desperate for anything to keep Cyneria safe; they would sell her off like cattle if it meant a stronger military. What would happen if he married her? Morana would not leave her; she would be forced to bear his children. Bile rose in her throat. As soon as she accepted his offer to marry her, she would be surrendering her sole control of Cyneria; she would no longer be the queen who ruled; she would be a queen who bore him children.

By the time she heard the servants come to announce the prince's arrival, she had worked her head so full of anxiety that her hands were shaking. She had not eaten breakfast, and her dinner the night before had been inside her own bedroom. She could not face Emris.

The servant made sure she was well-dressed. The white dress flowed around her ankles, and the corset pulled tight enough to accentuate her chest. She looked in the mirror for a long moment, with a gold pendant around her neck and pearl earrings in her ears. Her brown curls fell down her back, slightly pinned up by a conch clip at the back of her head.

The servant helped her down the stairs. She made her way to the throne room, hands shaking slightly. Guards wearing dark blue armour with gold stood at the bottom of the stairs, and then she saw him.

Her breath hitched.

From his letters, she had assumed he was a scrawny prince, even ugly. Valerie stood at the bottom of the stairs and caught his eye. His slightly brown skin stood in stark contrast to his almost silver eyes. Black hair fell in curls around his face. A white sash crossed his chest, held in place by a golden plate. White pants fell to his ankles. Silver rings adorned his fingers, and a smirk tugged at his mouth. Dimples appeared on either side of his cheeks.

As she slowly approached him, he dropped into a low bow; then she nodded respectfully. He was still a prince. Her guards stood beside him, watching as the two nobles stood in silence for a moment.

Then Castiler took a step forward, and she stifled her urge to flinch as he reached for her hand, the hand Emris had kissed. He brought his lips to her knuckle. His hands were slightly calloused, and the faint white scar from his lip to his collarbone on the right side of his face did not detract from his beauty.

He stood slightly, letting go of her hand.

"It is a pleasure, Majesty, to meet you at last," he said, his voice smooth with a slight southern accent. She allowed a small smile to touch her lips.

"A pleasure indeed," she replied politely. She took a deep breath before she gestured behind him.

"Join me?" she asked, and he nodded, extending his muscled forearm to her. She tucked her arm into the crook of his elbow, and he smiled softly before walking with her towards the doors. The gardens unfolded before them, and he took a deep breath. For a few minutes, she remained silent, unsure what to say. Was it normal for men to have so little to speak about with women they wanted to court? She wouldn't know; no man had ever displayed an interest in courting her.

The guards trailed behind them a few feet. She kept walking, but her mind wandered to Emris, who had walked with her in this same garden. Her gaze flicked to the willow tree as if she would find him lounging there.

"Is it always this beautiful in Cyneria?" He finally asked, and she met his gaze, those silver eyes staring through hers.

"Yes, the summer months are nearly at an end, although our winters are not nearly as cold as Lunivere's," she said, and he smirked.

"It truly is a beautiful kingdom," he said, and she nodded. Cyneria had always been a beautiful kingdom, and Linra was its prized jewel. She did not know whether he would appreciate her humour, so she did not attempt to make a joke.

"I have heard many stories of the alcoves of Dramira," she said, and he let out a knowledgeable grunt.

"Yes, most of those stories are true, I am afraid," he said, and she felt her head flutter slightly. It was not the feeling Emris gave her; it was more light-hearted.

"Of sirens and singing whales?" She teased, tightening her hand on his arm slightly, and he let out a throaty chuckle.

"I would rather you come see for yourself," he replied. She flushed slightly and met his gaze.

"Sirens would pale in comparison," he said with a low, sure voice. He was flattering her, and it was working. Her mother had always told her that she was a bright girl.

Sirens were rumoured to be the most beautiful creatures after faeries; some said they were even more hauntingly beautiful. She met his eyes, and those dimples were on his face again. She enjoyed his presence somewhat. She did not know why she felt a wrongness in her chest. Morana had not bared her ugly head, and she did not seek out the goddess.

How would she explain that to him? Would she describe it all? Would he be able to make him believe her?

It didn't matter, she told herself, because she wouldn't accept his formal proposal.

Her hand twitched in his grasp, but he didn't seem to notice.

Valerie tried to convince herself that marrying him would be the best choice. When the time came to accept him, she should do it. She would wear a crown like his, bear him children, and share a bed with him until they were old and gray. But an unsettling feeling curled in her gut at the thought.

As traitorous as her heart was, she knew that if it came to it, Castiler was not the man she would want to wake beside.

By the time dinner arrived, the prince had spoken of his kingdom and of everything except her. She felt her chest tighten. She sat down at the table beside him, her hands clenched in her skirt once more. Her conversation with Emris had boiled down to announcing him as her lover, and Castiler had to accept it.

Her jaw clenched as she watched the dining hall doors. Castiler continued speaking, but she faded from the conversation when Emris stepped into the room. Her breath hitched. He wore a white ruffled shirt and white trousers; his hair was perfectly done, and his eyes met hers across the space; amusement flared deep in his gaze.

She swallowed when she heard Castiler stop speaking, his attention fixed on Emris as he approached the table. When he reached the seat, he bowed low.

"I do not believe I have had the privilege of meeting you," Emris said, his head bowed to the prince, who looked between Valerie and Emris for a moment.

"Who is this?" Castiler asked, not noticing Emris, who had now risen to his full height again. Valerie swallowed, looking down at her plate. Emris slid into the seat beside her, and she felt heat flare in her chest. Emris, as if sensing her discomfort, turned to the prince.

"I am her lover, your Majesty," he said, and Castiler cocked a brow before raking his eyes down her body. She felt indignation flare in her chest. Emris had basically thrown the fact in his face, and if it bothered him, he might protest. But he had no power here in Cyneria, not yet at least.

"Pardon my shock, I did not know Her Majesty had a lover," he said, looking back at Valerie as if the idea was impossible.

Emris chuckled softly, and he met the princess's eyes across the table.

"She does not speak of me often, I am afraid; I don't seem to leave an impression," he said, and she flushed a deep red. Her hands twitched in her lap, and she raised her head to look between the two men. One asking for her hand and the other hiding her secret.

As if perfectly on cue, servants poured into the room, setting food down in front of the three of them. She took a moment to compose herself.

The prince seemed to be quiet for a moment before he turned to her, his eyes slightly softer.

"I suppose this would not be a good time to discuss our courtship," he said, and she nearly choked on her water. She glanced at Emris, who kept eating as if he had not heard them. His words burned into her head.

I am no worthy suitor or prince, and I know that he will give you everything you desire. But I want to be the only one you give your heart to.

She flushed but turned back to the prince, who was watching her warily.

"No, there is no better time. Please continue," she lied through her teeth. She could almost sense Emris' tense beside her. It was not uncommon for queens or nobility to bring their lovers into their marriages; sometimes, it even helped the marriage flourish. She knew this was not the case. The prince set down his fork and cleared his throat.

"In recent months, more faerie scouts have been spotted on our border, as I know you are aware of. Our courtship would provide not only military stability but also ensure the strength of a bloodline," he said so diplomatically. She felt upset. Wasn't a courtship supposed to be romantic, done for the love of another, not just for safety? She turned to watch him, her lips pursed, and for a moment she considered spitting at him, but instead she merely smiled softly.

"Prince Castiler, has a woman ever told you she would much rather be courted for her face or even her character, not for her military?" she asked, and she heard Emris laugh softly. Her heart pounded in her chest at the sound. It could unmake her in an instant. She feared she had struck a nerve, but the prince laughed.

"Believe me, your Highness, I would still ask to court you. You are a marvellous woman, and if your mother had not sent me an inquiry about our union, I would never have thought we would court."

She dropped her fork, and it clanged against the plate. For a moment, the world faded. It wasn't possible. Her mother had never tried to marry her off. Never. How could she do this to her? After screaming in her ear about the importance of leading a strong nation, she now wanted to sell her off like cattle. Had she really had no faith in her own daughter?

Tears shot to her eyes, and she quickly pushed back from the table.

"I'm sorry, would you please excuse me for a moment?" She asked, voice shaking, she felt tears burn her throat. Castiler nodded as if solemnly, but Emris only watched her hand twitching briefly under the table.

She left the room in a hurry, her corset suddenly constricting, and she made it to her bedroom as tears burned her throat and she started to breathe heavier. She felt rage at her dead mother.

Months ago, she had believed she might make a good queen, able to rule or marry whomever she pleased, but no, her mother had always doubted her. She slammed the door shut and stumbled into the center of the space, tears streaking down her face as she bit her lip hard enough to taste blood.

"How could I have been so foolish?" She spat in anger, her hands clenching into fists, she told herself she had to calm down, Morana would flare, she would-

The door opened on its own accord, and footsteps stopped inside the doorway.

"Valerie," Emris' voice cut through the quiet, and for a moment, she debated collapsing into his arms, but she merely sniffled softly, her hands shaking. The anger built inside her like a flame; she rubbed her eyes with her palms. The door shut behind him, and he crossed the room in seconds. She moved away, trying to hide her face in her hands.

"You should go back to dinner," she said, her voice breaking slightly as her pain clawed at her chest. She tried to wipe her eyes again, but he stepped closer, those eyes burning into hers.

"I would never let you break alone," he said, and she flinched as if struck. She finally looked up into his eyes, her face flushed and glassy from tears. She could not form words to explain. How could she explain anything to him? There was nothing she could say that would make her believe he wasn't deceiving her. He took a step closer, his hands reaching up to grasp her wrists. She tried to pull away, but he merely looked at her flushed face, his eyes softened even though his brow was furrowed.

"I do not expect you to tell me anything; I cannot demand your own story from you, but I am here," he said firmly.

For a moment, everything else faded; his thumb grazed her palm.

"Was it what he said?" he asked in a voice suddenly dangerously serious, his hands tightening slightly, and she nodded. He let out a sharp breath.

It took her a moment to swallow her tears. She did not look at him as she started to speak, her pain overflowing.

"My mother never believed I could rule like the queen she wanted me to be. My father was the only person who ever believed in me, and after his death, my mother belittled me for years. I spent so long trying to prove to her that I could be a good queen. She had told me she loved me, that I was enough, yet I was only her pawn," she said, her voice angrier now, tears flowing down her face. Tendrils of darkness flowed slightly from her fingers, but Emris did not flinch.

"She had promised me I would not need to marry to secure my throne; she had promised me I would be free from marriage. And now I hear this," she said, her voice cold.

"I hated her in life, but now in death I know not whether to mourn her, thank her, or wish my father had lived instead of her," she choked out. He said nothing, and it killed her. She dropped her head into her hands, and he released her wrists.

"She made me a monster, she made me watch her murder thousands of innocent people simply for what flowed in their blood, and then she turned me into her puppet," she choked out, and then she felt his hands on her shoulders.

She lifted her head slightly and met his eyes, her breath hitched at the pain in them.

"You are not your mother," he said firmly, and she shook her head. He merely took her chin in his hand and tilted her head, so she was forced to meet his eyes.

"Death is an untimely enemy, Valerie. I have seen more people die before me than live. You are not a monster for what she forced you to do; you are your own creature. No one can make you into a monster, not your mother or even Morana," he said firmly, and her lip quivered slightly.

Tears streamed silently down her face.

"We are the monsters we make ourselves out to be," he whispered, and for a moment, she understood what he meant. It should have scared her to think he was a faerie in the flesh, that he could snap her neck without thinking about it. But at that moment, he cradled her heart in a way her mother never had.

"You are allowed to hate, Valerie. You are allowed to feel everything towards her that you do because you did not deserve that," he whispered fiercely, and she let out a sob.

"If the gods spare me for however long they decide, I will continue to remind you that you are not a mistake and that you are most certainly not a pawn." He made her look at him, and his hand entwined with hers.

"You are a queen, with or without a throne, without Castiler or with him by your side." He whispered. Her heart cracked open as he spoke, and for a moment she could only look at him.

His other hand wiped the tears softly from her cheeks, his breath ghosting over her face. She swallowed thickly. He let out a sharp breath as if seeing a beautiful creature for the first time, and she cocked her head slightly in question.

"You are beautiful," he breathed, voice filled with awe, a rare laugh flitted from between her lips.

"Even when I am tear-stained, and my ribs are bruised from my corset?" she asked, and he smiled, a dimple appearing on his cheek.

"Especially then," he whispered, and for a moment, he leaned in as if to kiss her.

She did not know what to do; she had never been kissed before, and-The cat lounging on her bed meowed softly, drawing her attention away from his lips. She let out a breath she didn't know she was holding. Emris wiped a remaining tear from her cheek and then smiled softly.

She did not remember squeezing his hand, only that he squeezed back. He moved towards the door.

"Rest, I will inform his highness that you are unwell," he whispered, and her heart ached for a moment. He reached for the doorknob, but her voice cut through the quiet,

"Goodnight," she whispered, her hands clammy, and she resisted the urge to wipe them on her skirt. He turned to her, his eyes soft.

"Good night, Valerie."

Not Your Majesty, or Your Highness. Valerie. Her name. Something intimate he used to say that made her stomach flutter. She allowed herself to smile before he slipped out of the room, leaving her heart pounding so loudly in her chest that she found that breathing had become almost impossible.

Chapter 30

Emris wandered down the halls before informing a servant that Her Majesty was not feeling well and would no longer attend dinner. The girl nodded and hurried away to inform the prince.

Emris had disliked him from the start. Yes, he was handsome, but something about the way he raked his eyes down her body had made Emris tense. He could not get the sight of her tear-stained face out of his mind, nor could he erase the sound of her frantic heartbeat from his ears as he had leaned closer.

Gods, he had been so close to kissing her that he had trembled with restraint. He tried to convince himself that he had to focus on that if he was caught off guard, Morana would sneak up on him, but-

The memory of her shadows spilling from her fingertips and touching his hand was soft, not the blade that was Morana. No, they were from Valerie. An extension of her need to be seen, held.

Gods, her words had hit him so hard in the chest that he had nearly dropped to his knees right there. How could her mother do such things to her? Valerie was worth every kernel of love she could have. Emris clenched his jaw as he made his way to his room, the door shut behind him, and he ran a hand down his face.

Her previous hesitation around him had faded, and he assumed she had deemed her worries as unimportant.

He shrugged off his shirt, tossing it onto his bed. He barely made it three steps towards the balcony when a flash of pain hit his head.

It wasn't Morana, no, it was Ciro. His god had been quiet over the past few days… but now…

Emris' knees buckled, and he doubled over, hands hitting the cold stone. Pain

It flashed so sharply behind his eyes that he let out a groan of pain. He lasted a few more seconds before he hit the ground.

Emris lay on the grass when he stirred, his head no longer throbbing. Ciro had never seen him in person; this was different. The god stood in a meadow surrounded by green hills. He pushed himself up from the ground. He saw him so rarely that for a moment he did not recognize him.

The god was taller than him by a few feet. His eyes were a bright blue, and his high cheekbones were dusted with golden-white freckles. His muscular form was hidden beneath a white garment, and a crown of leaves sat on his head.

Emris stood and did not bow. He had stopped bowing to gods long before he had become a conduit.

Ciro watched him for a moment, his hawk perched on his shoulder. Emris had not seen the bird in months. It had always flown high above or perched in a nearby tree, but seeing it now sent his head throbbing.

"What do you want?" Emris asked, his mind once again caught on his encounter with Valerie. Her tear-streaked face had twisted his heart as if he had been stabbed through the chest.

"Cold, are we?" Ciro asked, his voice lithe and seductive, almost. He took a step forward as the wind blew the grass around his feet. The sky above them was filled with white clouds.

Every god had a different realm. Where Morana's was that of darkness, Ciro's was that of light.

Emris wanted to give a snarky retort but avoided pushing the god any further. Ciro was more lenient with Emris, treating him more as a son than a vessel. When Emris was first chosen as a conduit as a young boy, he did not know what fear was. Ciro had made him consider hurling himself off a cliff more than once, but over time, he had become his closest companion.

Emris levelled the god a glare, and he lifted a brow. Ciro clicked his tongue.

"Always so impatient," he said and stepped forward again. Emris did not flinch as the gods' glowing hand reached out and touched his temple. The vision unfolded before him in an instant.

The room was the same alabaster he had grown used to. The floors were white, streaked with gold. The space was quiet.

And on the throne sat a woman. No, a goddess.

Her face was Morana's, but her body was Valerie's. In her left hand sat a dagger, and in the other, shadows wrapped around her palm. Her black gown fell to her ankles, and her eyes were the same brown as they had always been, but dark veins now appeared on her hands and around her eyes.

Emris was shaking by the time he sagged on the grass. He felt bile rising heavily in his throat, and he doubled over. His face was pale, and his hands were shaking. The horrors he had seen were enough to stop his heart dead in his chest.

"Do you see why you must be careful of her?" Ciro said, slowly circling Emris like a predator. Emris could not find the words to describe what he felt. She had been so timid, so small, almost crying tears that were of sadness and grief- but in that vision, he had seen nothing but the bloodlust of a conduit fully possessed.

"When will this happen?" He choked out, pressing a hand to the ground to stabilize himself.

"I do not know," he said, as if he could not decide whether to tell Emris or not.

Ciro knelt before Emris then and cradled his jaw as he forced him to look at him.

"One thing is for certain: whatever game Morana is playing, she will not be lenient for long, she will consume the human queen, and she will destroy our world as we know it."

Emris was shaking then, his eyes squeezing shut, and Ciro dropped his face.

"Can't you stop her?" He asked, not sure if he meant Valerie or Morana. Was there really going to be a difference in the end?

"Morana is too powerful in her realm. I cannot reach her," he said, and a chill raced down Emris' spine at the realization. He stood straight, shaking slightly.

"I no longer wish to speak with Morana, Emris," he said, and his eyes met Emris'.

"I wish to kill her."

The words hit Emris like a blow. He knew nothing he could say would oppose his god; he would force him if he had to.

"What are you saying?"

Ciro looked at him for a long moment, his eyes scanning Emris carefully.

"Patience," Ciro said, as if aware that any wrong word would shatter his already teetering resolve.

In a moment, the realm faded out of his reach, and he appeared back in his body, his head throbbing.

He could not get the vision out of his head. Every vision Ciro had given him came true. With that thought, Emris collapsed into the bathing room and vomited into the basin so many times he could barely rise from the floor before sleep claimed him.

Chapter 31

Valerie had slept. For the first time in days, no nightmares had followed her into unconsciousness. Her hand was slightly curled into the blanket, and an ocean breeze softly slammed against the windows. She slowly opened her eyes, and as rain clouds gathered on the horizon, she smiled. She had always loved the sound of rain on windows.

Slowly, she uncurled herself from the pillows, her curls slightly messy. Her heart fluttered in her chest at the memory of the previous night. She knew it was stupid to think anything more of his touch, his words - but something inside of her wanted to hear his voice again.

The cat meowed quietly as she slid out of bed, her bare feet padding softly on the floor. Her heart fluttered in her chest as she made her way to the balcony, her hands running through her hair haphazardly.

Her mind was calmer than usual, no voice in her head, just the feeling of being understood for once. Emris had not looked at her with hatred the night before. He had looked at her as if he had understood her.

Yes, he was a faerie, and he had lied to her, but he had never wanted to hurt her. She had to believe that. Her heart gave a tug as she remembered Prince Castiler was still in the palace.

Quickly, she dressed in her usual blue silks, ran a hand through her curls, and tied them in a braid down her back. Her hands were clasped in front of her stomach as she made her way out of the room and towards the dining hall. She knew that Castiler and Emris would be at breakfast.

The thought of him sent a flurry of butterflies fluttering alive in her stomach. The table was bedecked with beautiful tableware, three plates set with her in the middle. Castiler was already waiting; she bowed gracefully towards him. Emris sat directly across from Castiler, his face more solemn, and it caught her off guard.

As she sat down, she noticed Castiler was smiling very friendly.

"I am glad to see you are feeling better," he said with a start, facing her more fully.

He was handsome, yes, but compared to Emris, he was- Well, they couldn't be compared.

"I am sorry if what I said last night upset you. I didn't mean to," Castiler began, but Valerie offered a polite smile.

"It is alright. I was feeling rather lightheaded." She laid her hands, tightening in her skirt. Emris sat there like a statue, unmoving, and she wasn't sure he was breathing. When she finally turned to look at him out of the corner of her eye, he seemed almost afraid.

Her jaw clenched. There was terse silence before Castiler spoke once more.

"I know it must seem extremely abrupt of me, and I hope it does not come across as a decision made without reason, but I wish to court you," he said, and her entire body stopped functioning. She knew that was why he was here; he had expressed as much in his letter, and yet it hit her in the chest like a blow.

She opened her mouth to reply with something polite, but Emris sipped from his water and turned his attention to the prince. She felt the hair on the back of her neck stand up. She shot him a look not to be rash.

"What makes you so certain Her Majesty would want to court you?" Emris purred, his whole attention fixed on the prince. She did not know whether he was trying to defend her or was proclaiming emotions he had hidden earlier. The prince shifted his focus to Emris as if suddenly disgusted.

"I am sure her Majesty can speak for herself," he said, voice low, and Emris didn't flinch; he looked between Valerie and Castiler.

"May I have a word with you?" Valerie asked Emris, who looked shocked, as if she even wanted to leave the prince's presence. Emris nodded nonetheless, and they left the room. She bowed her apologies before making their way to the gardens.

When they were finally alone, she felt her anger flare at his retort.

"How dare you?!" she said, and he looked her over once, leaning back against the willow tree.

"How dare I what? Speak up for yourself because you can't?" He snipped, and she felt her gut fill with dread. Was this the man she had thought of so whimsically that morning? Every butterfly in her stomach curled and died.

"Are you implying I am useless, that I cannot speak for myself?" Anger flared across her face, and she narrowed her eyes at him, daring him to speak.

He scoffed at her, and she took a step closer.

"I am implying that you have spent so long living for others that you have never cared about yourself," he said, sounding just as angry suddenly. She felt tears burn behind her eyes. She hated how right he was.

He took a step forward, his voice rising.

"You may think yourself helpless, that you must accept his proposal and obey Morana. You are not indebted to anyone but yourself, and you can't see it for the life of you," he said, his hands waving slightly as if to show the space around them.

Her anger boiled over. He knew next to nothing of what she had suffered in the past few months. Had not understood the hatred she had not only for her mother, but for herself.

"You assume it is so easy for me just to do whatever the hell I want," she spat, and he flinched slightly as if she had really struck him.

"You have no idea what I've been through this past year. You have not had a crown thrust upon you; you have not been degraded by your own mother for years, sitting there helpless." She was yelling now, angry as she walked closer to him.

"You know nothing of what it means to hate what you are because of your mother."

She spat at him, and his eyes softened a fraction. She stepped back from him for a moment, flashes of red behind her eyelids.

"And to think, I really thought you, of all people, would understand," she said with a small, bleak laugh, stepping back further. She turned to walk away, but his hand enclosed her wrist.

She tried to pull free, but he spun her until her back hit the tree trunk. The grainy knobs dug into her back, and she was disoriented for a moment before she met his eyes. He hovered over her, his face inches from hers.

"Do not run from me because you fear something within yourself," he said softly, letting go of her wrist.

"I know what it is to hate, and I know that no matter how hard you try to convince yourself you are worth nothing more than a crown or a vessel, I see who you are," he said.

She inhaled a sharp breath.

Rain began to patter down from the sky; they were dry under the willow tree, but the sound drowned out her breathing.

"If you wish me to go, I will go, Valerie; you need not suffer because of me," he said,

"What makes you so sure I am suffering?" She asked, and his gaze flicked down to her lips. For a moment, she thought he might kill her, his hands would clamp around her throat, but instead, he simply looked at her.

"Because my heart aches as much as yours when I am without you for too long," he said, one of his fingers coming up to tuck a hair behind her ear. His finger lingered on her jaw for a moment.

How had she gotten there? Angry one moment and utterly infatuated with him the

"You shouldn't touch me. Morana might-…"

"Morana could kill me for all I care, because if I touch heaven, then hell is worth it."

She scoffed slightly as he continued to look at her.

He swallowed as if contemplating something to say.

"If I kiss you, will you have me executed by morning?" he asked, and her breath caught in her chest; she felt the butterflies return in a swarm. She had never kissed anyone before, and the thought of it scared her because of her vulnerability. His finger traced her jaw carefully, and her eyes latched onto his lips.

"We shouldn't," she said, but he did not move.

"Why not?" He asked, his brow creasing with amusement, that dimple appearing beside his mouth once more.

"Castiler might find us."

"As far as he is concerned, I am your very disrespectful lover." She met his eyes again, and her breath hitched.

"Are you afraid of me?" he asked in a voice softer than ever before. He watched her as if she were the moon and he was a lonely star.

"Shouldn't I be asking you that?" Her breath was hitching again, and her voice came out weaker than before. Her face was hot as he ran a soft finger down her jawline.

"You're blushing," he said, and she resisted the urge to snap back at him. She stammered out an apology.

"You look rather beautiful when you blush," he said. At that moment, all logic left her mind. She did not care if Castiler saw them, if Morana killed her. She did not care for anything except his warmth against her and the idea of kissing him.

"If I kiss you, would I regret it, Emris?" She asked, her voice soft, and for a moment, she saw him shudder as if her voice unravelled him.

"I would regret it if you didn't."

With that, he moved closer, took another breath, and pressed his lips to hers.

Chapter 32

Emris felt as if his entire chest had caved in the moment he pressed his lips to hers. The heat in his stomach curled into his chest. She pressed her lips to his tentatively, as if unsure how to move.

He smirked against her mouth before dropping one hand to her waist and threading the other through the sensitive curls at the back of her neck. She gasped against his lips, and something deep in his chest snapped. He pressed her more firmly against the tree's bark and kissed her deeply.

He had wanted to kiss her for as long as he had known her. He couldn't explain why, but he had the urge to be near her every moment of every day, as if she were in sunlight.

The vision Ciro had given him had been throbbing behind his eyelids all morning, and looking at her had been painful. But now-

He couldn't stop kissing her, and she couldn't stop kissing him. His soul was sparked alive, and for some reason, Morana had gone utterly silent. Her threats dissipated into the wind, and the sound of the rain pattering around them.

She made a slight noise in his mouth, and he swallowed it. His hand tightened on her hip, and she kissed him back harder. He didn't move to loosen her corset. He kissed her because a part of her soul called his.

She broke away first, and he gasped as air flooded his lungs once more. Her face was more flushed than before, and he looked from her lips to her eyes. She was smirking slightly, a soft smile that he rarely saw. Her face was calm and yet dazed as if she had thought about this moment for days.

His hands shook slightly, and as quickly as the vision had disappeared from his mind at kissing her, they flooded right back into his head.

Valerie stood over a pile of broken bodies, her face aghast. He took a step back, not letting his expression falter. She did not know about the vision, and he intended to keep it that way. For a moment, she looked at him softly, as if trying to decipher him. He bit back on the urge to reach for her again.

He hated how deeply she had entranced him. Every thought of the vision vanished when he thought of her lips. Could this be Morana luring him in? He took another slow step back and let go of her waist.

Her face dropped as if she understood it must have been a mistake. Dread curled in his stomach, and he opened his mouth to speak when the sound of rustling drew near, tearing her gaze from him. He turned to see the female guard who had come to visit Valerie running towards them. She slowed a few feet away and then bowed low.

Valerie walked past him slowly, as if he had not just kissed her breath, as if he could still not smell the vanilla and citrus on her skin. The dismissal stung in his chest, but he forced himself to try to focus on the two women.

The rain had made the guard wet; her black hair was slightly plastered to her head. She stood after a moment and turned to Valerie.

"We have news from the border," she said, and Emris watched as Valerie tensed. Emris did not know whether they meant the wall or the two neighbouring kingdoms. Valerie nodded, and the guard looked to Emris as if considering moving to a more private place to speak, but Valerie interrupted her train of thought.

"You can tell me here," Valerie said. He noted how breathless she sounded, her face still flushed. He forced his smirk to disappear as he beheld her standing there, utterly undone by him.

The guard nodded, then spoke.

"Some of our scouts found faerie archers climbing the wall; three of our men were killed in the altercation. They are planning something."

Emris tensed at the words. He refused to let his surprise show.

Without another word, Emris left the garden, his heart pounding in his chest.

Chapter 33

Valerie couldn't stop her heart from beating in her ears. The kiss had shattered her composure, but she forced herself to understand the severity of Seraphina's words. Her hands were clenched, and she felt her palms start to sweat.

Her friend observed her face, as if noticing her overly flustered expression.

"Have our sources revealed anything more?" Valerie asked. Her mother had hired assassins and spies to infiltrate various kingdoms. They were among the best; if they needed information, they would get it.

Seraphina shook her head.

"Many of them know it would be suicide to cross the wall in these conditions," Seraphina said. The lack of belief that they would make it out of this hit Valerie hard. She fiddled with a piece of lace on her skirt.

"I have spoken with General Arminia. She has suggested we send six spies to Krovaria across the wall, and to Dramira and Lunivere."

Valerie locked eyes in question with Seraphina, but the guard spoke.

"We do not know if another war is upon us. Dramira and Lunivere may not be our allies in the end," Seraphina said, and Valerie felt as if she had been struck. Prince Castiler sat in her dining hall, and she had just kissed a conduit faerie, as if he were her salvation. Her head spun.

If she took one wrong step, she would fall to her doom.

"What do you say?" Seraphina asked, and Valerie looked behind her to glance at Emris, but found him gone. Her gut tightened.

If she wanted to draw her own spies away from her and from the goddess lurking under her skin, she would need to distract them. The war might turn against them, and she had bigger problems to worry about. She raised her head slightly.

"Send them," she said, and Seraphina bowed respectfully. Before her friend could leave the willow shelter, she stopped her.

"And inform Prince Castiler that I wish to speak with him in my bedroom." The words tasted sour, but it had to be done. Seraphina did not question her choices as she bowed once more and left through the downpour.

Valerie felt as if she could not breathe. Her head was spinning.

She was a conduit for the goddess of death, the queen of Cyneria. War was threatening their borders, and she was falling for her enemy. She dug her nails hard into her palm and told herself she would need to forget Emris.

Valerie knew that was an impossible feat.

Valerie sat on the chaise in her bedroom, Castiler across from her on the twin bed. A cup of tea sat on the small round table in front of him. She hadn't touched hers. The rain still pattered on the window, and she found her words quietly before facing him.

He was already watching her.

"I would like to apologize to you. I have been rude in leaving you so suddenly. Please forgive my rudeness, and I hope we can discuss your proposal over breakfast."

At the words, he smiled slightly, his eyes soft now, his black hair falling in front of his eyes slightly, and he brought a hand up to push it back from his face.

"There is no need to apologize, Your Majesty," he said and took a sip from his tea before turning to her once more.

She felt all the air in the room being sucked up as he started to speak.

"I understand that our human lands are constantly under threat of war. The wall is growing thin, and while I would gladly say our kingdom is well prepared, I cannot make that promise. For thousands of years, faeries have tormented and slaughtered our people."

She nodded, all her history lessons coming to mind.

"Dramira can provide ships, cargo, and soldiers should a war be launched upon us." Valerie tensed slightly at the words. Seraphina's request to send spies into Dramira forced her to smile. He swallowed before meeting her eyes again.

"That is not the point," he said with a sheepish smile, and she remained silent, letting him continue.

"I have not known you long, have not known you at all, really, but the things I have heard about you are as extraordinary as you are. You are as cunning as you are beautiful, and any man would grasp at the chance to court you," he said, leaning forward slightly as if in a meeting.

"You flatter me," she said, her face slightly hot. But she could not see him; all she could see was Emris leaning to capture her lips in his.

Could she really accept Castiler? Emris was a faerie; he could not hide it forever. He was a powerful conduit. How could her people ever accept him as their king? The thought struck her hard in the chest. Should a war break out?

If Emris agreed to marry her, they could change the law. The idea fluttered to life in her chest, and her eyes widened in slight excitement, but she remembered where she was. And those dreams were as foolish as her dreams of sailing away.

"I know I must seem terribly sudden and desperate in asking for your hand," he said, and as he stood from the couch, she felt her hands tremble. He removed a ring from his pocket.

"My father welded it when I was a boy," he said, and she examined the silver thorns that curled around in a circle.

"You do not need to say you will marry me, for that is a big commitment. But can you at least agree to be courted by me? If this war comes between them, I will wait," he said softly.

She looked at his face.

She knew he loved the version of herself she showed to people, the queen who had everything under control, the perfect ruler.

She looked at the ring.

If Emris had done this, would she have said yes more easily?

She shoved the thought deep into her chest as she looked at him, eyes soft, then she nodded. His smile split into a grin, and he reached for a hand. She placed her fingers into his palm, and he slid the ring onto her ring finger.

Castiler leaned down to brush his lips over her knuckle.

"As much as I would like to stay here in Cyneria, my father has summoned me back," he said. He let go of her hand lightly, and she forced a smile, standing beside him.

"It has been an honour, truly," she said, trying to capture the excited feeling of a woman being courted, but could not find it in herself. He bowed once more.

"Until we meet again, Your Majesty," he said as he rose. She bowed her head respectfully, and he slipped out of the room. His guards escorted him out of the palace.

Her heart dropped to the soles of her feet, like a rock plummeting to the ocean floor. She looked at the ring that sat so heavily in her hand. She wanted nothing more than to tear it from her finger. She clenched her jaw in silent anger.

What would she say to Emris when he noticed the ring? She sighed, her hands resting on her hips for a moment. She bit her lip, considering the lie.

You owe him nothing.

Morana's voice cut through her head, and she flinched slightly, her heart beating faster. Morana had been scarce of late, but Valerie no longer feared her as she once had. She did not know whether that made her brave or foolish.

She hated that Morana was telling the truth.

If he hides his identity from you, then you can hide this. Lie to him.

She sighed and bit her lip before accepting the truth. Because she had a bigger problem, Valerie left the room, leaving the tea to cool on the table as she headed towards the library.

Because if Emris was a faerie and the wall was being scaled-
She realized that she might have made a terrible mistake.

Dust had gathered on the pages of the books. She stacked a few of
them on the floor and curled up against the shelf. She needed answers.
Her father had loved to learn about the faeries.

Her mother had thought it silly to teach their daughter about the
monster-like creatures, but her father had spent hours telling Valerie
about the beasts.

She flipped open the first book, and her throat almost closed with
tears. Her father's winding handwriting was in the first margin of the
text. She swallowed her grief and kept flipping.

Her father had told her the truth, nonetheless, about what the faeries
really were. Valerie flipped through until she found the section labelled
'Creatures of evil'.

Her heart skipped a beat. Her mother had burned nearly every book
about faeries since her father was killed. She had only found the books
because she had hidden them. Her father's writing was in all of them.
She glanced at the small stack of five books beside her, adjusting the
candle a few feet away.

She flipped the page once more and found heavily descriptive text.
Her father's words were written in the margins, underlining and circling
specific words and phrases.

Although the younger generations knew very little about faeries,
their ancestors had suffered firsthand at the hands of the faeries. They
had been slaughtered and tortured for years. Many claimed that
surviving Priestesses or merchants had written books about the faeries.
Her father had tried to get his hands on as many of them as he could.

He had been a king and a general, yes, but part of him loved to learn about things that were out of his reach.

She flipped the page, scanning for anything that might explain the faerie kingdoms better. She huffed a sigh, but her eyes latched onto a piece of paper sticking out at the side of the book. She flipped to the page and found a neatly folded square of paper. Tucked away against the spine of the book. She tugged on it carefully.

The edges were slightly frayed, and she had to unfold it slowly. The paper crinkled under her fingers. When she saw what it was, she almost gasped. The map was unlike anything she had ever seen.

She stood carefully for a moment to unfold it completely. She set it down on the ground and placed a book in each corner to keep it from folding in on itself. Her heart pounded in her chest.

All the maps in Cyneria depicted the human kingdoms with detail, trees, mountains, rivers, valleys, and towns. The faerie kingdoms had been left with only the name, but this-

The map depicted the faerie lands so beautifully that one might expect the gods to have drawn it.

The wall's thick line cut the continent into two. She traced the line with her finger. Farthest north, across from Lunivere, sat a small cluster of islands in the same oceanic sector as Vecuria. She read about the many landmarks. The dunes that spanned the kingdom conjured images of a vast beach in her mind. Cliffsides cut through the border between Vecuria and Krovaria. A palace with a name written in a faerie dialect was sketched near the center of the kingdom. Valerie could almost feel the sun beating down on her.

She turned her attention to Krovaria, and her chest tightened. Seraphina's words flashed through her mind once more, and she felt her chest ache. The kingdom was a lush green land, depicted with many lakes and rivers that cut towards the ocean in swoops and dips, and a large white palace with another unreadable name sat on a hilltop. Four small towns are nestled between the borders of the lands on either side of the kingdom. Her hand skimmed over the name.

Listeria sat at an angle beneath Krovaria, its coast curving to border Saelia. Listeria was darker than the rest of the faerie kingdoms and was covered entirely by the Rocky Mountains. There was no hint of green, and she felt a shiver run down her spine. It was bleak and bland. Valerie felt as if the darkest creatures would crawl forth from those mountains.

Her eyes travelled to the kingdom beside it. Saelia was depicted with harbours spanning the entire coast, two smaller islands nestled within them. The blue of rivers and the green of grasslands meshed throughout the small kingdom. She spotted the palace further along the coast. Her father had always said that sirens were rumoured to swim from Saelia towards Dramira.

Valerie studied the map for another moment, her chest tight. If her mother had ever found the map, she would have burned it. How many of these maps remain in Cyneria? She left the map where it was and slowly moved to sit against the shelf again. She skimmed through the book once more; her hands flipped quickly through the pages. Many of the servants had retired or were having dinner in the servant hall. She doubted anyone would find her; she was in the darkest part of the library.

Her ring caught the light again, and her chest tightened. She kept skimming but found nothing useful.

I can show you.

Morana's voice purred. Valerie considered denying the goddess, but the goddess knew more than Valerie did. She nodded, and before she knew it, the candle blew out in a breeze, and she slumped to the ground.

The space around Valerie was no longer the darkness she had grown so accustomed to. Instead, it was a white space that unfolded in every direction. She did not know where she was, so she waited. Morana walked towards her, back in her original form. She did not flinch at the goddess, and Morana seemed pleased.

Then she spoke.

"Long before your world, there was a time when only the gods existed. They did not need to rule over anything; they simply were. Then some of them grew tired of having nothing to rule over. They wanted to be revered," she said, and with a sweep of her hand, the entire room flooded with gods, so many that she could not count them all. They all appeared as humans, made of black mist.

"So, we created the faeries first. Made them beautiful and dangerous, into a race so powerful they could destroy each other for their loyalty to us," she said, walking past Valerie to show her another figure. The gods faded away, leaving only Emris standing there. She shivered, and he disappeared in an instant.

"For hundreds of years, they thrived, and we got the praise and fear we had always wanted. But we grew greedy for more power, so we created humans," she said, and with a wave of her hand, a baby made of mist appeared in her arms. Watching Morana hold the child was unsettling.

Had her mother held her the same way?

"They lived shorter lives and knew they were weaker, so they depended more on us for what we were." The baby vanished from her arms. The space around them grew darker until it was black.

"We gave them power, so much of it that they could see our divinity. We gave them choices and cities crafted from diamonds and gold. Wine flowed from cups," she said bitterly, then turned back to Valerie.

"The faeries grew selfish over time; they didn't need us; they needed power. So, they slaughtered as many humans as they could. Many of us were angered by their stupidity and withdrew our power from among them," Morana said, and Valerie remembered the first great war.

"Only a few of us chose to create conduits. To live out our will in Milornia." Morana said her emerald eyes were once again focused on Valerie, just as the cats were.

"You wish to know more about the faeries," she said, and Valerie nodded. She remembered the kiss with Emris.

"Is it because you have grown to love one?" Morana asked, and dread filled Valerie. She did not know if she loved Emris; she did not know what love was. Valerie opened her mouth to lie, but Morana stepped closer, and her mouth fluttered shut.

"You are a puzzle, Valerie. You are a human queen, my conduit. Your mother has stirred enough hatred for anything remotely powerful that you would be murdered within hours of your discovery. Faeries threaten your land, and yet you have given your heart to one."

"I have not given my heart to anyone but myself," she snapped, and Morana levelled her a glare.

"You truly believe that?" Morana asked, her voice softer, almost contemplative.

She reached out and stroked her hair away from Valerie's face.

"You have fallen for him," she said, gazing into Valerie's eyes. But she swatted Morana's hand away, shaking her head as if she could not accept it.

"I do not blame you, child. Faeries are hard to resist. We made them alluring." Valerie spun on Morana again, her anger hot in her stomach, coiled like a snake ready to strike. She did not know how Morana could stand there and judge her.

"What do you suppose I will do then? Just accept him and hope that he doesn't want to murder me in cold blood for his people?" She asked, her hands shaking slightly. She hated that tears burned behind her eyes.

Morana took another step closer, her eyes more solemn.

"Do you want an answer?" She asked, her voice serious once more, and Valerie nodded.

"Loving a faerie is bound to doom you, whether you admit it to yourself or not. He is immortal, and you will live if I command you to. Even if you somehow escaped your duties and ran away with him, your womb would carry more children who will be oppressed than if you married Castiler."

Bile rose in her throat, and tears started to track down her cheeks.

"If you want to secure yourself, keep your people safe, you will stay far away from the boy," Morana said, and Valerie took a sharp breath. She had grown used to his presence, to his witty remarks and his bashful smiles.

Morana took another step and cupped Valerie's jaw, forcing her to meet Morana's emerald eyes.

"I will not stop you from choosing him, but you know nothing about who he really is. Tread carefully."

With those words, the realm faded out of her vision. Valerie blinked awake on the cold stone floor. The candle was still burnt out, but light had started to trickle in through the windows. She sat up, head throbbing, as she hurried to pack away the books. She stuffed the map into the pocket deep in her dress and stacked the books behind a small alcove where she would find them again.

Morana's words haunted her as she made her way back to her room.

Your land is threatened by faeries, and yet you have given your heart to one. You have fallen for him.

Valerie did not think about anything other than those words as she slammed the door to her room shut and collapsed on her bed. The cat curled around her ankle as if it understood the grief of loving someone who would doom you.

Chapter 34

The dream came in whispers. However, Emris could not tell whether it was a vision or a figment of his imagination.

The small house was filled with the sound of laughter, the infectious laughter of children bustling to and fro. Emris was sitting on a large chaise, sharpening a small wooden dagger he had spent months carefully crafting. The hearth was warm and filled the space with light.

A small boy no taller than his knee sprinted into the room, his brown curls bouncing as his wide golden eyes spun around the room. The faintly pointed tips of his ears caught in the light as he barreled for his father.

The boy was laughing as he wrapped his short arms around Emris' torso, barely coming around him.

"What are you playing, little warrior?" Emris asked the boy who smirked that bashful grin Emris himself had worn for so long.

"Sera is chasing me," he said, his voice small and wistful. As if on cue, a little girl toddled into the room. Her brown eyes stood in stark contrast to her white hair, which was pulled into two small pigtails on either side of her head. She wore a beautiful yellow sundress and toddled in, smiling with a gummy grin. The boy darted away, and Emris set down the small sword before standing.

"There's my little princess," he said and bent to scoop his daughter into his chest. She giggled and squealed as he planted kisses on her face and neck. He placed her down gently, and she uncurled her fingers from his before toddling after her brother.

Emris walked towards the kitchen, where the smell of freshly baked pastries was filling the air. He leaned against the doorframe and beheld the scene.

Flour, sugar, citrus pieces, and thick icing were concocted in a few bowls-

There in front of the small hearth, she stood. Her hair was done back in a braid, brown curls shining in the morning light as her hands moved to taste a pastry. She turned.

Her stomach was round with their third child. Her brown eyes met his.

Emris was shaking when he awoke in a cold sweat. His head throbbed, and he gripped the sheets as a sob broke through him. The image of her swollen with their child, two children running around a house-

He stood without thinking, his hands shaking as he made his way to the balcony. He ripped the doors open, and the cool early morning air slammed into him hard enough to knock back the waves of nausea.

His bare chest heaved heavy breaths as he clutched the balcony railing. It couldn't be true.

The first vision had been clear, her destroying everything with Morana using her as a vessel. But this-

Emris did not know whether it was a vision or a dream. Ciro had told him that sometimes, depending on the choices someone makes, visions can shift, but they would come true no matter what the outcome. Dreams were something he crafted with his own will.

Had he thought about her in that way? Imagined her with their own children? He shuddered and lost a shaky breath.

Before his father's illness had clouded his mind, he had told Emris the story about the Soul-Bound. As a young boy, he had thought nothing of it, tales to get him to sleep at night. But when he had reached manhood, his father had told him again.

The Soul-Bound were those whose fates were woven together by the gods themselves, fated to be one.

The memory sent another shiver through him as he dropped his head into his hands. She couldn't be his Soul-Bound. Only faeries could be Soul-Bounds; anything else was just regular love or attraction.

His head throbbed as he swallowed, breathing hard. He lifted his head to gaze out at the harbour. A few boats were setting out to sea, while a few lanterns burned in the town below. The water glistened in the early morning light.

When he had first become a conduit as a young boy of twelve, not even into his early years of manhood, visions had haunted him. Some concerning the death of his mother, some nights she was alive, others she was dead. When she had been assassinated months later, he knew it was his fault.

His father had known he was a conduit, not through a priestess but by consulting a healer to find out what was wrong with him. Months later, his father was bedridden.

Which version would come true?

Valerie, standing above dying men, destroying the world with power that should belong to no one? Or with her as the mother of his child?

The next morning at breakfast, he waited for Valerie to come downstairs. He had arrived early, sitting in his usual seat at the long table, fiddling with his knife. He could not think about anything other than the image of the little boy hugging him around the waist.

His mind was full of questions, and Ciro was nowhere to be found. When Valerie descended the stairs into the dining hall, his breath caught in his lungs. Their kiss flooded back into his mind, alongside the image of her pregnant with his child.

He cleared his throat and met her eyes across the space. She wore a beautifully crafted green silk dress with slits on either side of her thighs to allow for movement. Her arms were covered entirely by sleeves, and her hair was curly, falling down her back. She met his eyes, and his world slowed. He forced all his emotions out of his head.

She looked away as if embarrassed, her face hinting at a faint flush. She looked devastating, with or without a crown, with or without his children.

He swallowed thickly as she sat down, forcing himself to look down at his plate so he wouldn't linger on her lips again. The kiss had undone him; even thinking about it made his pulse spike. They were silent, and then she spoke.

"I'm sorry for kissing you," she said, and his head snapped up. Her lips were pressed together, and she looked away from him, as if ashamed. Heat rose in his chest, and a slight anger thundered in his head. Did she not know how long he had wanted to kiss her? How long had he tried to claim her?

"Don't." He said firmly, and her eyes met his. The anger that had made home in her eyes had slowly receded into a softer emotion, one that made his heart skip a beat.

"Do not apologize for something so unbecoming, Valerie," he said firmly, his hands flexing on his trousers.

Her eyes latched onto his lips again, and she lost a breath as if relieved that he felt the same.

"Do you regret kissing me?" "No."

He found that he was not lying. He had not regretted it. The visions hadn't mattered; all that mattered was that she had kissed him back like he was her salvation, and for a moment, all the gods and their demands fell from their minds like stars from the sky. Her cheeks pinked again, and she cleared her throat, reaching to sip on her water.

He knew something had changed in her. He could sense it. Her guard had reported faeries making their way towards Cyneria.

Emris' jaw clenched slightly.

Even if his people sieged the entire kingdom, he would never regret kissing her.

That frightened him more than Morana.

Chapter 35

Valerie did not know why she had decided to visit Linra. She also had no idea why she had invited Emris to join her. The carriage ride was quiet. She sat opposite him, their knees brushing. She tried to forget their earlier conversation, when he had so blatantly declared that he hadn't regretted kissing her.

Her hands fidgeted with her skirt. Emris was gazing out the window, and occasionally his eyes would flick back to her, even though she pretended not to notice his attention.

The sun had come out from behind the clouds, and in the distance, the ocean glistened under the heat. The driver stopped them in the town square, and she hesitated for a moment before opening the door.

The ocean air and a mixture of fresh bread and fried fish hit her all at once, and for a moment, she felt at peace. Children were playing with a ball in the street as vendors chatted ceaselessly. No one seemed to notice her for a moment, which was a reprieve.

Emris rounded the carriage to stand beside her. She tensed before she melted into his presence. She wanted to reach for his hand but knew better than to cross that line again. He had kissed her, yes, but he was also a faerie. She had to remind herself of that.

Slowly, they started to walk away from the carriage. His golden eyes were soft as he looked around him, observing the children, vendors, and homes with clothing lines dangling in the breeze. The sun was almost blinding.

One by one, people started to notice her as they walked. She swallowed her paranoia as she bowed respectfully to women and children. She felt a stifling urge to disappear from Linra at that moment. She walked towards the docks, Emris trailing behind her.

The early morning was filled with the clamour of nets being unstrung and sails being pulled back. The wooden planks of the harbour were full of fishermen, and on the glistening water, ships sailed towards the horizon. Her heart suddenly felt lighter.

Emris strolled beside her, his hands in his pockets; his face was calm. She met his eyes as they stood near the beach.

"It's beautiful," he said, gazing out at the ocean, his voice velvety as if soothed by the sun.

A sudden sadness constricted in her chest, and she forced it away. Her father loved sailing with her when he did not have a council meeting to attend. Before she knew what she was doing, she extended one hand towards him. He looked down, and without hesitation, he took it. His palm was warm against hers, his larger, lithe fingers curling around hers, and she felt that flutter in her stomach.

"I want to show you something," she found herself saying, and he nodded before she gently tugged him with her. Not once did he let go of her hand; his thumb brushed over the back of her knuckles. She remembered Morana's warnings, and yet something inside of her wanted desperately to forget them.

The wind blew as they approached the cliffside, the steps wide enough for them to walk side by side. Slowly, they climbed, and after a moment, he spoke.

"He gave you the ring, didn't he?"

She stiffened. She had forgotten about the silver band on her finger, and she tensed slightly, the urge to pull her hand out of his grip almost overpowering.

"He did." She found no strength to lie to him, and she glanced at him. His brows were drawn tight suddenly. He knew her responsibility, didn't he? She shoved the thought away as they climbed. They reached near the bend on the mountain, and she glanced down. Sharp rocks jutted out from the water, reaching for the sky like hands. One wrong step and they would both plummet.

Fear coursed through her instantly, and her hand tightened in his. She led them past the cave where she had so often found solace, leading them towards the bend in the cliffside. Valerie had rarely visited the pools.

On the other side of the harbour, cut off from Linra in a sense, the coast was shallower, allowing small pools to form, black rocks cutting paths through the shallow water. Her heart thundered. Why had she wanted to show him this?

Carefully, they made their way down until their feet touched sand. Slowly, she pulled her hand from his and felt the cold breeze bite into her palm at the loss of heat.

She looked to see him flex his hand as if remembering that it was his once more.

Slowly, she reached down to undo the laces of her boots. She slipped them off easily and let her bare feet touch the sand. A flare of heat traced up her spine.

Very few people ever wandered to the pools, too afraid to brave the steep cliffside, and not finding it worth the effort to sail there when the ocean was open to them. The sun made her skin feel deliciously warm. For a moment, she forgot about Emris and felt everything around her.

Her skirt tumbled around her feet as she slowly padded towards the water. The salt of the ocean hit her in the face, and she found herself laughing at the beauty of the water before her. Gulls cried from above, watching as she neared the water. Seraphina would implore her to be careful, Jezebel would shriek at the thought of getting the dress wet, but Emris -

She turned to find him watching her as if entranced. Their eyes were locked for a moment before he bent down to pull off his shoes. Her heart fluttered again, and she turned as he rolled up his pants.

She bit her lips before stepping into the water. The tide rolled in slowly, crashing over her feet and sinking them deeper into the sand. She smiled slightly as the peace washed over her.

She had shared this spot only with her father before he died. She did not feel sad in that moment; instead, she took another step forward. The hem of her dress soaked up the seawater like a sponge, and she felt a laugh building in her throat. She waded deeper until the ice-cold water reached her knees, then she scooped up water in her hands. She threw it into the air and watched as the droplets fell back to earth.

She laughed.

She hadn't laughed honestly in so long that she felt it with her whole body as it escaped from her lips. She clutched her stomach as she spun in the water, arms thrown up as she laughed again, head tipping back to feel the sun on her face. When she was left gasping for breath, she turned back, and her breath caught.

Emris had walked into the water, and he only stood a few feet away. Her heart fluttered at the softness in those golden eyes.

"Dance with me," he said, wading closer, and she felt another laugh bubble from her lips. He watched her as if she were a goddess.

"We're in the ocean, Emris," she said with a laugh, turning around again to gaze at the horizon. The wind tossed her curls over her shoulder, and she pushed them back, her face splitting into another smile as she turned to him.

"I would dance with you anywhere," he said, and she felt her heart skip a beat.

Slowly, she waded towards him, and even though she knew she shouldn't, she placed her hand into his. The water crashed around their legs, the current nudging them towards shore, but their feet dug into the sand.

They stood there for a moment before he guided her one hand to his shoulder, the other still in his palm. His hand slid to her waist, and he pressed close. She met his eyes, tracing his face. That feeling from kissing him flooded her senses again at that moment, but she did not turn away from him.

If she kissed him again, would her heart be his? Or had she already forfeited it before that day?

Slowly, he began to take steps with her in the water; they moved in a circle, the water dragging at her skirt, but she didn't care. He watched her with such a soft expression that her dimples were faint beneath his skin, and her brows were no longer creased.

"Did he ask to court you?" Emris asked, and her breath hitched. She stopped moving in the water for a moment, but she forced her face to be calm. For a moment, she felt tears burn behind her eyes. She did not want to forget this or allow it to fade away.

"Emris?"

"Yes, sweetheart?" She lost her breath.

"Can I ask you a favour?" "Anything."

She sighed and met his eyes, aware that tears were gathering behind her eyes, and if she didn't speak soon, her heart would spill over once more.

"Can we just forget about everything? The court, the ruse, the gods. Can we dance here for a little longer? Please." Her voice cracked on the last word, and he smiled softly before pressing a kiss to her temple. She let her head nestle into the space between his chin and his collarbone.

He did not answer, but he swayed with her there, his hand still on her waist and her face buried in his shirt. The soft cotton dug into her face, and she closed her eyes. Valerie didn't care if he was a faerie or if he had another identity; he cradled her like she was something precious. That was something her own mother had never even done.

He smelled intoxicating, and she wondered if that was his natural scent. Faeries tended to smell more delicious, often like a pastry.

The water was a lulling presence, and she leaned her head more fully against his chest, his chin resting on her head. Even though she could feel every nerve in her body melt against him, Morana's words rang in her head,

If you want to secure yourself, keep your people safe, you will stay far away from that boy.

Her breath hitched, and for a moment, she hated Morana. "Hold me a little longer?"

He chuckled softly against her head, "Always."

Chapter 36

After they stood there swaying in the water, they moved to the beach. Her skirt was sodden, and she hated how it clung to her ankles. Sand stuck to her wet feet as she began to look around. Shells jutted out of the sand, and she felt like a child once more as she moved to pick them gently out of the sand.

Emris sat a few feet away, propping himself up on his hands as he watched her. It felt surreal, like a dream.

Everything else faded away as she looked for shell after shell, slowly making her way towards the water to rinse them off. After gathering a handful, she moved to sit down beside him. He seemed at peace.

Faeries were deadly and dangerous, but here-

Emris smiled softly as she sat down beside him, and he ran a finger over her curls. She tensed but allowed herself to accept the touch. The question of what they were lingered in the back of her mind, but she shoved it away as she set the shells out in front of her.

One was a light blue with swirling patterns looping towards the center. Another had a pinkish hue, covered in small white specks. She could not count how many times she had returned to the palace as a little girl with shells so plentiful they could fill jars.

After a few moments of laying out the shells, she cast them back into the water and lay down on her back. Crossing her ankles. It didn't matter that her dress would be utterly covered in sand. The sun was hidden slightly by the clouds, and she pressed her hands to her stomach, breathing deeply as the waves crashed a few feet away.

She didn't have to open her eyes to know that Emris was watching her.

"You're staring," she said, eyes still closed, earning a chuckle from him.

"Does that bother you?" He gave his voice a deep, velvet tone. She finally opened her eyes to meet him. He sat up slightly, one elbow braced on his knees, while the other leg was stretched out beside hers. In the sunlight, he looked even more devastated.

She shook her head, trying to hide her flush. She had so many questions that she felt she might overflow. But she knew that as soon as she opened that door, it would never close again.

He observed her quietly for a moment, and she felt lighter under his stare. Castlier's eyes had made her feel tense and stiff, but Emris had a way of making her melt without touching her or speaking.

She grasped the sand under her, playing with the grains as they fell through her fingers. She did not remember him leaning over her, but she did remember him pressing another kiss to her lips that decimated her thoughts.

And for a moment in time, she knew that she would never forget that moment. The two of them tangled on the beach, laughing and dancing as if nothing mattered.

As if the gods were not watching so closely.

By the time Valerie had washed all the sand out of her hair, the sun had gone down. Casting Linra in darkness. Her head throbbed slightly from the sun, and her cheeks were warm from the heat.

The flutter in her chest had not stopped.

Not since Emris had kissed her again, smiling against her mouth. Her fingers traced her lips as if remembering the touch. Her hair was still wet when she pulled on her nightgown and robe. Her hands grasped the candle as she slowly made her way back to the library.

She could not forget the memories of earlier in the day, but she had a duty, nonetheless. The cat trailed behind her, a quiet presence as she opened the doors to the space. The candle wobbled in her other hand. She held it steady as she slipped into the room, the cat following closely at her ankles.

The candle cast light across the library, and servants had already retired to their rooms as she walked quietly through the aisles. She reached her small corner at the back of the room and sat down, the cold stone biting into her bare legs. Her hands trembled slightly as she reached for the books she had hidden. The cat purred as it curled over her knee and climbed into her lap. It nuzzled into the space, and she did not flinch. Although Morana had revealed to her more than the books had, she found herself drawn to the secluded pages.

She set down the candle and flipped open one of the books while simultaneously petting the cat.

Hope had clawed at her chest in faint whispers. Would she be better off fleeing to the faerie lands if a war were coming? Would the faeries take her and make her a revered?

Would Emris steal her away to wherever he was born and marry her? The thoughts felt utterly traitorous. She was a queen, a human queen. She could not forsake her lands for a faerie. Her people would be slaughtered.

Valerie knew what she felt for Emris was real, whether she admitted it or not. She needed to know whether he felt the same and, if he did, whether he would spare her if his people reached Linra.

Her hands shook slightly as she untucked the map once more, laying it out in front of her for another observation. Her eyes traced the borders between the faerie lands, and her heart ached. If she had been born a faerie, would they have taken her in?

The thought stirred longing in her chest. If Morana was always fated to pick Valeric, maybe she could find a home on the other side of the wall. The thought felt foolish, and she regretted even thinking about it.

Emris still did not know she knew what he truly was. And she intended to keep it that way. Whatever had been built between them had to be real. If it wasn't, Valerie didn't know what she would do. Did she seriously believe that love between them would be possible? That somehow, they would find a way to love each other, right?

Tears burned in her throat.

He was everything she should never have. A faerie, something her mother had hated in life. He was too intelligent for his own good and too powerful to be safe. Morana had nearly killed him the first time he got close and had warned her to stay away from him.

A shiver traced down her spine.

A part of her would always love Emris, she realized. No matter which prince courted her for an alliance or who she ended up marrying, he would always have her heart tucked into his hands.

If she somehow found the strength to confront him about lying to her all that time, would he turn on her like she feared he would? Would he kill her, admit that whatever they had shared was a ruse and a game just to get her off the throne?

Valerie knew that if that were the case, Morana would shield her. Valerie let her head fall back against the bookshelf, her eyes squeezing shut. In another life, she was never meant to be a queen; she was just a girl deeply in love with someone impossible to chase after.

Chapter 37

After hours of staring at the map and feeling tears build behind her eyes, she rose and made her way to the palace gardens. The cold wind bit at her through her robe, and she wrapped it around her tightly. The darkness did not part for her; instead, it wrapped around her as she walked.

Fireflies danced across bushes and flower petals as she walked slowly. Her mind was far away. What would her mother say if she knew what her daughter had become? A conduit and someone who loved a faerie? A bitter taste filled her mouth. Her mother may have been responsible for her existence, but Valerie doubted she had ever loved her as a daughter. Even if she could have explained it all to her mother, she would have killed Emris that night of the gala.

Arminia still wrote reports concerning the different executions performed almost daily. The letters were left on her desk, and whenever she returned to find one, she would cast them into the flames.

She knew she could speak to her advisors, convince them that she was queen, and killing innocents would not aid them in winning the war. She knew that, did she not?

She rounded one of the hedges, walking deeper into the maze, when she spotted him. He was leaning against a sculpture of a woman holding a babe. His golden eyes fixed on her, and he smirked. Her stomach did a flip as she stopped walking.

Her mind was just as full as it had been, and yet she felt the edges softening as he strolled closer, hands in his pockets.

She met his eyes, and he smiled softly.

"Can't sleep again?" She shook her head.

"Thought I would get some fresh air," she said. She knew she should remember what he was, challenge him, and demand answers, but she couldn't, not when her heart ached at the mere sight of him.

He slipped in beside her and walked with her. She remembered them kissing on the beach, and her chest tightened. Did he love her, or was it all a game? She knew better than lingering too long on the question.

The night air swept around them, the sound of birds and crickets filling the silence between them. They reached the edge of the garden, and she could make out the ocean over the finely trimmed hedge. He had stopped beside her, hands stuffed deep into his pockets.

"Do you think we will win this war if it comes to it?" She asked and turned to look at his face. He faked a perfect smile and nodded.

"I think you are stronger than you let on," he said, stepping closer again, towering over her.

She felt her stomach flip, nonetheless. That warning from Morana flared in her head again. If she wanted to save her people, she had to stay away from him and yet-

Before she could move, he protruded his hand from his pocket. She met his gaze as he dangled a thin silver necklace between his fingers. The pendant at the end was one of a small shell. Her heart tugged painfully.

"I know I cannot offer you a ring or a palace, or the life you truly deserve." He started stepping closer, looking down at the pendant.

"But if he can offer you a ring, I can offer you this," he said, pressing the necklace to his chest over his heart, and she felt tears build behind her eyes again. Then he gently showed her the necklace, and she traced her finger over the shell.

"Where did you get this?" She asked, her voice thick with emotion. He smiled softly and scratched the back of his head, as if thinking, but his voice came out sure.

"I went back to the vendors when you disappeared after dinner," he said, and she felt her heart clench as her eyes squeezed shut. She knew she could not accept something so beautiful. To anyone else, it would mean nothing, but to her, it meant everything.

She took a step back, her eyes meeting his. His smile fell as he beheld her expression. "What's wrong?" he asked, suddenly aware that something was amiss.

"I can't take this," she said, her hands clenching in her robe. He looked almost hurt but took a step closer.

"Why not?"

"Because it means more than a necklace," she said, and he flinched slightly when she met his eyes.

"I am well aware of that," he said, not harshly, as if already aware she was hesitant.

"You cannot give this to me because you cannot promise me you will stay," she said, and her voice cracked on the last word. His eyes softened slightly, and he swallowed thickly. She told the truth in a way he could not decipher. If he found out she knew his identity, or if his people came for him during the siege, he would not be able to stay. But that did not frighten her as deeply as the thought of losing him because of herself. She knew he feared Morana, even though he pretended he didn't.

He stepped forward, and she swallowed again. He spoke once more, voice determined.

"I cannot promise you I will stay, but I can promise you my heart," he said, reaching for her fingers and pressing them to his chest above his thundering heartbeat, close enough that she could feel his breath on her face.

"This heart will go with you no matter where you tread," he said, and his hands shook as he watched her head. He could not say these things and lie to her; the words wanted to bubble out of her mouth, but she shoved them down.

She wrenched her hand out of his grip, and the necklace went limp in his other hand.

"I cannot love you, Emris," she choked out, tears blurring her vision. She wanted

She loved him so dearly, but fate would not allow it; her gods and his people would never allow it. She would not survive if he turned against her.

He took a step back and scoffed; the pain was unbearable.

"So, you kiss me, and enchant me, and now suddenly, you cannot love me?" He asked, shocked and visibly hurt. She felt anger flare, but she did not allow it to show. He had a right to be angry, just like she did.

"You dare not to love me because you know that if you let yourself be loved by *me,* you would never be alone again," he said, and the words were so truthful she bit back a sob.

He stepped closer again, his hands trembling now, his face pained. In that moment, she believed he really did love her, or at least he had. She was looking at the ground now, her hands clenched. Her heart was thundering in her chest. She wanted to go back to the beach and drown in the memory of his lips on hers.

"I have been foolish to think you could ever choose me," he said, and she felt the bite of his words deep in her chest. He stepped back, but she felt tears building again.

"I thought you cared for me, Emris," she said, her voice cutting through the air as tears burned down the sides of her face, and her lip quivered.

"I thought maybe you wanted me, not Morana, and that you would see me," she said, her fears laid bare. She waited for him to strike, to call her out, to yell at her, scream at her, but he looked at her as if she had unwrapped the stars with her hands.

He swore low and stepped closer.

"I thought that too. For so long after I arrived here, I convinced myself that maybe I could come for Morana, speak with her, let Ciro speak with her, and be gone from this place. Back to my home," he said, and she felt her tears growing. He stepped closer, his hand tucking a curl behind her ear.

"I deceived myself into thinking I did not need your voice or your warmth. That I did not crave your snarl or your biting words in the early morning," he said, his voice pained, and for a moment she froze.

"My heart has been yours long before I knew it," he said, swallowing thickly, and she let out another sob.

"And I know he is better for you. More well-suited than I can ever be," he said, his hand grasping his chest as if it hurt, "but some part of me wants to steal you away from all this forever. But I could not ask you to forsake your crown or your people, I could not ask you to let yourself be dethroned for *me*." His voice cracked, and at that moment, she realized that she loved him.

She stepped closer and grasped his hands in hers; they trembled in her grasp, and her tears blurred her vision, but she looked at him, nonetheless.

He wiped a tear from her cheek, and his touch lingered.

"You are a queen, and I am-"

"Everything." She choked out, and his eyes met hers. She felt more tears streaming down her face. She knew that they could never love each other right. Her advisors would never let them wed, and even if they did, Morana had warned her.

"Oh, Valerie," he said, his voice cracking on her name once more, and he reached for her hand, kissing her palm. She met his eyes again and felt as if she was drowning anew.

Her mouth opened, and her breath caught; she wanted to utter those three words. Those three words that would shift everything between them. But she couldn't. She stepped back, her chest constricting, and he met her eyes in question.

Her hands were shaking. She had to cut him off, had to forget him before she said she loved him and ruined everything. Before she allowed him to keep her heart.

"I cannot love you," she said finally, and his eyes welled slightly; the sight took her so off guard that she almost apologized. He stepped closer.

"No, no Valerie-"

She took a step back from him.

"I will not love you, Emris." She said it louder now, sharper, as if set in stone. His breath caught, and he swore again, low, his hands clenching hard enough that she saw the anger in his jaw.

"Valerie, *please.*" He begged, his voice cracking, and she thought he might fall to his knees before her to beg at her feet. She swallowed the burning in her chest, the pain in her gut as she turned to him, eyes suddenly cold.

"I want you gone by dawn," she said. Her voice shook, and his breath caught. He stared at her, pain in his eyes, and then they softened as if he could believe it. He moved closer, grasped her face between his hands, and kissed her hard.

She pushed against his chest but kissed him back, nonetheless, her tears mingling on his skin as she made a slight noise into his mouth. Then she shoved him back, her heart aching as if someone had torn it from her chest.

"Valerie, don't do this." He begged, and she shook her head, eyes squeezed shut.

"I'm sorry," she murmured, and before she knew what she was doing, she was running back to the palace. She made it to her room with her head throbbing. She did not remember slamming her door or screaming into her pillow.

Did not remember anything other than his words. He loves *me*.

He loves *me*. *He loves me.* He *loved* me.

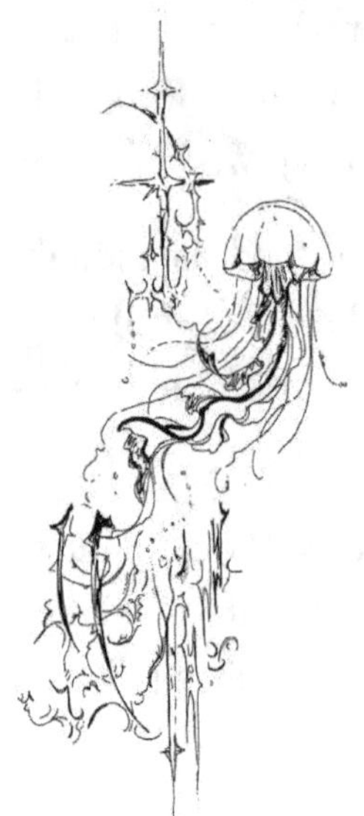

Chapter 38

Emris made it back to his room, choking on his emotions. He felt rage so deep in his gut that he slammed the door shut and sank one of his daggers into the wooden dresser. He was panting, breathing in rage, seeing red behind his eyelids.

He had been a fool. An utterly deluded fool.

He slammed his fist into the wall, feeling the pain lancing through his arm, and he grunted as he spun back towards his bed.

How could she?

How could she do this?

He had kissed her on that beach, proclaimed his love and loyalty to her, and she had just cast him away as if he was nothing. His chest ached, and he dug his hand into his pocket, fishing out the necklace. He stared at it for a moment.

Emris knew he had been foolish to fall in love with a mortal. He knew that even if she somehow found out he was immortal, she would hate him. Her people were going to be slaughtered by the other faerie nations, yet he had somehow thought he would be different. That she would love him. He had been so close to telling her, so close to saying that he loved her.

The gods be damned.

His head throbbed as he dropped his head into his hands, gripping his hair so hard it hurt. He hated that he still loved her. That he had seen her tear-streaked face and wanted nothing more than to court her right there. That was why he had bought the necklace.

He knew it would mean nothing to her, and yet he wanted to offer her his heart in earnest. He would give her nothing more than fear and grief if she knew who he was. But he loved her. He still did.

Before he could reconsider, he was out of his room and stormed down the hallway, convincing himself that if he just spoke to her, told her the truth, she would learn to love him, learn to…

Pain slammed into him, coursing from his jaw to his toes. He collapsed, hands clutching the carpet. His head throbbed.

"Not now, *please,*" he begged, but Ciro pulled him under faster than he could utter her name.

The realm opened in front of him like a lily pad. He stood there in the glen, his hands balled as he stood from the ground. Ciro looked angry.

The sight caught Emris off guard.

"You are a fool." Ciro spat, moving closer like a predator assessing prey. Emris resisted the urge to flinch at the words.

"She is Morana's conduit; did you not see the vision?" Ciro asked, and Emris levelled him a placid look.

"Do you mean the one where she was the mother of my children?" He bit back his voice harsher. Ciro didn't give in to the bait.

"That could be one of hundreds of possibilities." "And yet it was one of them."

Emris was almost yelling, rage still coursing through his veins. Ciro looked unimpressed with his bouts of anger.

"I should have told her who I was," he said, and the rage that consumed Ciro's features made Emris flinch. The god was across the glen in moments, gripping Emris' collar but not pulling him.

"You are an idiot. I am your god, and you will do as I command you. What would have happened if you told her and got yourself killed?" Ciro spat, his eyes glowing with near-erupting anger.

"Who would have been there to…"

The words caught in Ciro's throat, and for a moment, dread coursed through Emris'

body.

"Would have been there to what?" He demanded, and Ciro stepped back, letting go of his collar. Fear coursed through Emris.

"Been there to what?" He demanded, shouting now, his voice filled with rage. "To kill her."

The words hit him so hard in the chest that he felt as if he could not breathe. His hands were shaking, and for a moment, he felt as if he could not draw a breath. Was it true?

"I would not have brought you here to Cyneria, for me to speak to her Emris, you must have known that."

Emris barely heard the words; his heart was pounding so loudly that his ears had flushed red.

"The vision was clear: that she would become a monster that none of us can control," Ciro said more gently.

"And what makes you certain the other visions are false?" Emris rasped out his eyes, burning.

"You would risk the fate of our world for her womb?" "No, for her heart."

Ciro laughed once more, and it was bitter.

"You forget your place, Emris," Ciro said, his hands weaving golden light as he stepped closer.

"I have brought you here for no other reason than to kill Valerie. As soon as she dies, Morana will flee her body, and I can kill her once and for all. You would save the world."

The words were so bitter that, for a moment, Emris felt anger and rage. He wanted to shield her from his god. Protect her.

"I will not save a world where she is not in it," he said, and Ciro's eyes hardened again.

"You do not have a choice," Ciro said, and Emris felt the blood drain from his face. "No," he said, but Ciro continued to walk closer. Before he knew what he was doing, he turned and ran, forcing himself to wake up, slamming himself against the barrier of the realm.

"*No!*" He was shouting now, begging in his heart for this to be another wicked dream, another nightmare.

He was screaming for Valerie to run so loudly that he did not feel Ciro touch the back of his neck and have darkness claim him.

He awoke on the ground. Emris tried to push himself up to reach her, to call out to her and tell her she had to run.

Ciro had done something every god could do to their conduit. He had inhabited him.

His mind was his own; yes, he would watch everything unfold before him. But he could do nothing. He felt his mind recoil as Ciro shoved him off the ground. Emris began begging Ciro to leave her alone, but the god didn't listen; instead, it returned to Emris' room and sat there waiting.

Emris wanted nothing more than to die. He knew no one could hear him, but he whispered words he hoped the wind would carry to Valerie.

I'm sorry. I'm sorry. I'm sorry.

Chapter 39

Valerie awoke with her hair plastered to her tear-streaked face.

Her eyes had only shut the night before from exhaustion. She hadn't stopped crying. She had hoped that the finality of her command would have brought her peace, forcing her to accept that he would never be the one she could have.

She rose slowly, the sun shining through the windows as she rubbed a hand over her face. Valerie knew going down to breakfast was useless; if Emris had truly loved her, he would also have listened to her when she had told him to leave.

She would never see him again.

Something hollow opened in her chest as she rose, her hands still shaking. She rubbed at her puffy cheeks and forced herself to breathe. Now that he was out of the way, no matter how painful it had been, she did not have to worry about his motives. Whether he had told her he was a faerie or not, it did not matter; he was gone. She knew her soul would mourn him for a long time.

But she could not focus on him now, as much as she wanted to. She had a war to win. Before she could let herself sink back into her bed, she called for a servant and had her assemble all her advisors in the council room.

She just prayed she would not see Emris on the front lines when all hell broke loose.

Valerie arrived in the council room with dread in her stomach and a hole in her chest. She felt as if her entire heart had been sucked out of her body. Dimitrius sat still, as usual, his hands fiddling with one of his silver rings. Arminia looked completely ashen. Valerie knew that look. Her mother had worn it often, after she got used to all the murders.

Callus sat on her right, observing her as if she might explode. Tears still burned behind her eyes, and she had had to wash her face twice to make it look as if she hadn't sobbed into her pillow all night.

She waited for a moment to calm herself.

"It has come to my attention from General Arminia and Seraphina that faeries have infiltrated our border on the wall," she said calmly, and the three pairs of eyes fixated on her. She swallowed, refusing to look away.

"General Seraphina has reassured me that all threats will be neutralized, and in the case that more faeries are seen crossing the wall, we must start to prepare for war." The words were tense and final. Callus looked deeply unimpressed, but she continued.

"Cyneria is allied with Dramira and Lunivere in case of a siege. Our trade routes must be secure and remain that way to ensure our resources do not wither."

She felt like her mother, speaking to her council in a political tone. Arminia spoke next, her eyes tired and weary.

"More soldiers are being moved towards the smaller towns against the wall and are preparing to evacuate the towns should you give the final order."

Valerie nodded.

Arminia had more faith in her than she had in herself.

Had the general known about her mother's inquiry into having her married to Prince Castiler? Surely, she would have told her.

Dimitrius cleared his throat, but her eyes did not turn to him as he spoke.

"Has the alliance been sealed officially between Dramira and Cyneria?" he asked, his voice was almost too interested.

She bit back a retort, her chest aching.

She could only remember how Emris had offered his heart to her, and she had shoved him away. She fidgeted with the silver ring on her finger. Last night, in a fit of anger over her actions, she considered informing Castiler that she no longer wanted to court him.

But what difference would it make?

Emris was gone.

"The prince has asked to court me, and I said yes for the time being," she said with finality, not wanting to go into the great many things concerning the prince.

"What shall we do now?" Callus asked, and she forced herself to clear her mind.

Forgetting about Morana, and Emris, and everything she had thought she once had within her grasp. She turned to him, folding her hands and swallowing before speaking.

"We prepare our soldiers for war."

With that, the council was dismissed, and she stood with her chest hollow once more. If the faerie lands decided to launch an attack, Cyneria would have little chance of staying standing. The faeries had been quiet for so long that they could have been planning anything, and no one would know. Even their most skilled spies had come back with nothing or not come back at all.

She slowly wandered back to her room. Upon entering, the cat had curled up on the balcony, and she joined it. Morana had been quiet as of late, and it was a comfortable silence.

The wind bit at her face as she leaned on the railing, her hands tightly wrapped around each other.

She gazed out at the ocean, watching as ships slowly receded into the distance.

She hoped Emris had returned to his home, that he would find peace there, and that he would forget all about her and their time on the beach.

She knew she would have to.

Valerie knew that Emris was gone, that she should marry Castiler as quickly as possible to form a stronger alliance. It was only a matter of time until he proposed properly. She rolled the ring on her finger, closing her eyes with a heavy sigh. Would she ever be free from the will of others?

Seraphina had told her to be careful. Why had she not heeded her advice? Kept her hatred for Emris alive?

She groaned, letting her head loll between her shoulders.

The cat purred, rubbing against her ankle, its tail curling around her calf. The breeze played with her curls, pushing them away from her face. A chill seeped through her, and she felt as if it was meant to embrace her in a sense.

Then Morana's voice cut through her head.

You must leave, now.

A shiver shot down her spine, and she straightened.

What do you mean? Valerie asked, looking around her as if she were being watched. She made her way back into her room, the cat following close behind, and she shut the doors, locking them.

He is coming for you.

At the words, she stiffened, frozen in fear, but without letting herself stay that way for too long, she grasped her dagger from beside her bed, stuffing it into its sheath on her thigh. She knew it would most likely be useless. But she had Morana, did she not?

That's when the screaming started.

Valerie froze. It was that day all over again. She walked to her mother's bedroom to find her throat slit and her blood spilling out onto the silk sheets. Her stomach was clenched.

Who?

Morana didn't answer. The cat beside her hissed slightly as if it knew. She inched towards the door. The sound of screaming continued, and she swallowed her terror as she opened the door slowly. Had the faeries found her? Had the assassin come back to finish her off?

She opened the door fully and stepped into the hall. The sight that greeted her nearly sent her retching. Bodies were strewn, mainly those of guards who were stationed near her room. Her face paled. Who would do such a thing?

Then Morana's voice filled her mind again, firmly.

Run.

She did not hesitate. As soon as she heard the words and felt the hairs on the back of her neck stand on end, she was sprinting. Her skirt flew behind her as she ran, stepping over still-cooling bodies, her heart thundering in her head. She was running, the cat chasing after her.

She spun around the corner, then the next before…

Valerie felt all the air drain out of her body as she beheld the scene. Two guards fell to the ground as a sword cleaved through their chests.

She felt as if she were dreaming as she beheld him.

Those golden eyes were no longer soft but hard.

She felt as if she had just greeted death when Emris lifted his eyes to hers.

Chapter 40

She felt as if she were watching everything from above, her hands slack at her sides as adrenaline spiked in her chest. The cat beside her hissed. Emris just stared at her.

Those were not the eyes she had come to love.

His face was hard, and he showed no recognition as he slowly stepped over the bodies, not wiping the blood off his face as he slowly approached.

"Emris?" She asked, he approached her like a predator, and in that moment she understood.

He was here for her.

She couldn't open her mouth to argue with him.

Run.

Morana's voice was a shout in her head, and she blinked out of her daze. She turned and started to run. Her hair flew behind her as she sprinted back down the hall, the cat following close behind her. She did not know if Emris had given chase. She did not want to know.

The bloodlust in his eyes had nearly killed her.

She was running as fast as her legs would allow, lifting her skirt with her hands. She reached a stairwell, taking the stairs in twos and threes. She had nearly made it to the throne room floor when she felt Emris. In a moment, his hand gripped hers and slammed her into the wall so hard she swore she felt her skull crack. She was crying, then writhing, as she met his gaze.

"Emris, it's me, it's Valerie, please," she begged, her hands clutching at his wrist, now encircling her throat. He straightened his other arm, sword fully extended. She barely knew how to breathe as fear slammed into her. She was going to die, and he was going to kill her. The last thing she would see were those eyes that were not his.

He lifted his sword and prepared to strike, but she found herself closing her eyes. A scream of pain tore through the air as he was suddenly yanked off her. She gasped, sputtering as she choked on air flooding her lungs.

The cat had become something larger. She looked as the massive panther grabbed hold of his arm, sharp teeth digging in and ripping him from her. He stumbled back and hit the banister. For a moment, she thought he was hurt enough to stop moving. Then he looked up and smiled.

It was a smile that stopped her heart. That wasn't Emris.

The panther hissed a low, dangerous sound, putting itself between the two of them. She looked at him, feeling all those emotions crashing down on her. Was he here for revenge? Was he completing the mission he had been given all along? He lunged again, and the panther sliced at his leg with its massive claws, hissing again.

"No!" she cried as he fell again.

I warned you, child.

Morana said in her head, and she shoved the panther away. For a moment, she knew he would come back, so she did what she thought was right. She knelt there beside him and whispered, "Emris?" Her voice was soft, his head was slightly bowed, and he was breathing heavily.

"I love you," she choked out, and for a moment she thought he might have heard her. Before she could reach out to touch him, he grasped her hand and snapped her wrist. She screamed in pain and shoved herself back, clutching her wrist, tears springing to her eyes. The panther lunged, but a beam of pure light struck it, and it hit the stairwell hard with a crack.

She felt all the breath leave her lungs as he backed her up against the wall. She was sobbing now, clutching her wrist. Her back hit the wall, and for a moment, she felt fear deep inside her body. She was going to die alone.

Her body was shaking, she was crying, tears streaming down her face. Had her mother felt like this? Weak?

Emris reached for his sword once more, hobbling closer to her. When he opened his mouth, it was Emris' voice, but not his words.

"You will never be the destroyer, you will be destroyed," he said, raising the sword above his head, angled down towards her chest. She was shaking harder than she ever had before. She looked up at him with that pleading look, begging him to stop.

She barely thought at all as the blade slammed down, and she closed her eyes.

She waited for the blow, waited for the piercing of flesh and the feeling of life draining from her body. She opened her eyes and froze. Emris stood there, his hands suspended and caught.

The shadows had come, curling around him in the shape of large hands, holding him up as if he were a blade of grass. Her anger flared deep in her stomach, and with a flick of her wrist, the shadows shoved him.

His sword scattered to the ground as he was knocked back, his body hit the stone hard, and he tumbled for a moment and let out a low groan. The shadows curled back towards her. She was panting, gasping.

How could he do this to her?

He had said he loved her. Had it all been a lie? She stood, her hand shaking, her wrist already limp and swollen. She slowly stood, and when her body was fully upright, she beheld him there on the floor. Anger boiled low in her gut. He had lied to her, betrayed her.

Emris lifted his head, and the look in those eyes…

For a moment, she thought she was seeing things because the pain and fear in his eyes were unlike anything he had ever shown. He pushed himself up on one arm, his other bleeding heavily from where the panther had sunk its teeth into him. His eyes flicked around the room until she met him across the space.

The shadows curled around her like a second skin, twirling around her ankles as tears still streamed down her face.

Emris sobbed slightly, lifting his face to her, but she could not smile, could not breathe.

"I'm sorry, Valerie, I-"

"You do not speak in my presence," she said, her voice cutting through the air like a blade. She took a step, her wrist aching as she slowly approached him. The panther had risen, limping as it crept beside her, watching the crumpled mess of a man on the floor. Her rage boiled up so vigorously that, for a moment, she felt like her mother.

She beheld him, tears streaming down her face, in anger, not in fear. The guise had fallen away. And she beheld him fully. No longer rounded and petite, his face sharper, his body broader. He did not drop his head in shame, but her eyes narrowed on him, nails digging painfully into her palm.

"Has your god suddenly forsaken you, Emris?" She asked, her voice cold and hollow as if speaking to a traitor.

He opened his mouth to speak, tears brimming in his eyes.

"You have one chance to tell me who the hell you are before I slit your throat," she said, her voice ice-cold. His eyes widened slightly, but he swallowed his pride; his voice didn't falter as he spoke.

"Emris, Valerie, you know-"

"I know *nothing* about you," she screamed, and he flinched. Anger flared in her stomach, and the panther growled low beside her in warning.

"I will not ask you again. Who the hell are you?" She demanded as tears streamed down her face. She hated how her heart suddenly hated him. He had betrayed her, lied to her, tried to kill her. He swallowed thickly and did not try to hide his voice as he said loud enough for her to hear,

"My people call me Vandrill," he said, and she stood there shaking with anger.

"King," Morana translated.

Her stomach dropped to her feet. It couldn't be true; she couldn't have been so utterly gods damned stupid. Morana had never warned her not once-

"That means king," she rasped out and hoped he would deny it, but Emris lifted his head, eyes now clouded with an emotion she could not name.

"You are not the only royal, Your Majesty." She felt her heart stop beating in her chest. He had manipulated her.

"You lied to me," she bit out, and he opened his mouth, eyes soft again.

"You lied to me," she snapped, and the shadows curled around her hands. She sobbed again. She had truly loved him. He tried to rise, blood pouring from his arm.

The shadows whispered, and Emris heard what they said.

Some call him the King of devastation. But others know him as Emris King of Krovaria.

The words hit her so hard in the chest she staggered back, her uninjured hand covering her mouth. She felt tears stream down her face. She had been convinced he was another lowly faerie, not a king of all things. She felt her anger rise, and the panther snarled again, teeth bared.

She felt her heart shatter into so many pieces that she knew they would never be fixed. The sound of running filled the space, and her guards streamed into the room, Seraphina among them. She crossed the space and beheld Emris on the ground; his pointed ears and eyes fixed on Valerie. She turned her sword towards him, ready to strike should Valerie give the command.

She opened her mouth to utter it, to wish him out of existence before his voice cut through the fray as guards surrounded him from all sides, archers knocking bows from above.

"Forgive me, Valerie." His voice was firm, and she met his eyes across the space. The panther had transformed quickly back to a housecat, leisurely strolling as if it had not torn into his bicep like a piece of meat.

Before she could give the command, a blinding light filled the room, emanating from Emris. She was shoving her way past Seraphina, trying to reach him. She had barely grazed the side of his face with her palm when he vanished in front of her eyes. She staggered back, her heart burning in her chest.

His last words echoed deep inside her body. Her wrist gave another twinge of pain. Soldiers were now speaking, marvelling at what they had seen, others shouting with outrage.

Valerie remembered nothing.

Because as soon as she had seen him disappear, her heart tore open, and she felt the world tip as darkness claimed her.

Chapter 41

For two days after Emris disappeared, she didn't eat or sleep. Seraphina constantly checked in on her, sitting beside her bed and examining her broken wrist that had already started to heal. Valerie could not stop staring at one point on her wall, as if that one spot might provide solace.

Tears had not fallen since that day.

Morana floated in and out of her head, the cat curled in her lap. She did not think about anything other than who Emris was—the king of Krovaria, the kingdom that was starting a war.

She knew then she had been foolish to care for him. She hated him now.

By the third day, she had assembled all her advisors. She had been helped into her clothes, and she had not met the girls' eyes in the mirror as she tied her hair back. She sat at the end of the table, numb. Her hand throbbed, but she did not allow it to deter her from her initiative.

Callus, Arminia, and Dimitrius were bickering about the outrage it had caused.

"To think the queen's own lover was posing as a human, it's almost unbelievable," Dimitrius said, and she forced her anger to calm.

Rumours had spread like wildfire. The entire kingdom knew about Emris, about how he had been her lover, trying to get closer to the crown before he revealed himself to be a faerie and vanished out of thin air.

To many, it sounded impossible.

Valerie waited for the right moment to speak, her voice cutting through the air.

"Whether we want to bicker about my past lover or decide to try and find him suddenly, I can assure you that there is nothing we can do to stop the rumours."

The advisors went quiet at that, and she took the opportunity to speak.

"My mother fought hard to keep our Kingdom alive and thriving throughout her reign. She ensured our people were protected from faeries."

She swallowed.

"Taking into consideration the recent circumstances and the threat of war looming on the horizon, I have a direct order that has been discussed with the Prince of Dramira through letters as well as the king and queen of Lunivere." All three of the monarchs had agreed to her proposal.

Seraphina had assured them that the threat of doing nothing was greater than the threat of fighting back.

"The human provinces have declared war upon the province of Krovaria."

The room was so silent that one could cut the tension with a knife. Dimitrius was the first to turn to her.

"Are you mad?!" He nearly shouted, standing from his seat, one of the guards at the door tense, reaching for his sword.

"If we launch a war on Krovaria, the lands will ally and wipe us all off the continent. What you are proposing is suicide," he yelled, and for a moment, she let him have his moment in the sun.

"The next time you speak to me in that manner, I will have your head, am I understood?" She said, and he paled, sitting back down. She had been weak for too long, allowing her advisors to manipulate and use her as they pleased. She was not that queen anymore.

"Any other splendid ideas?" she asked, and the table was so quiet that she turned to Arminia.

"Prepare the majority of our forces to move out by the end of the month," she said, and the general nodded, placing a hand to her heart in reverence. Without another word, she pushed away from the table and left.

Her heart thundered so loudly in her ears that it almost drowned out Emris's thoughts about that moment when he had nearly killed her. Morana had saved her; she was due the respect she deserved.

That night, she sat in her room, her wrist now unbandaged and nearly healed. A long scar was evident on the back of her hand, curling over her palm. She felt nothing as she sat there staring at her hand, feeling the crushing strength of his fingers.

That same hand that had run through her curls or cupped her jaw. Morana pulled her under without announcing herself.

Valerie knew what she needed to ask the goddess. She knew what the goddess wanted from her.

She stood before her, eyes colder than they had been and no longer filled with fear or dread—only anger and rage.

She felt like her mother.

Something she had never thought she would become. Morana lounged on her throne, watching as Valerie stood there.

"I have a proposition for you," she said, and Morana cocked a brow, "Is that so?"

Valerie nodded, swallowing before taking another step forward.

"If you help me win this war, I will serve you until my dying breath." She had thought about this choice for three days. Felt how her anger had eaten her up until she could rarely blink without feeling rage.

"What makes you certain I cannot force you to serve me?" Morana purred, rising from her throne and walking towards her slowly.

"If I did it willingly, wouldn't it be more rewarding for you?" She asked, and Morana laughed softly.

"You offer what you do not understand," Morana said, reaching out a hand to touch her jaw. She did not flinch.

"I understand."

Morana looked at her as if contemplating whether to accept her offer. Then the goddess reached out a hand and pressed it to Valerie's back. Pain flared, and she doubled over as a feeling of unbearable pain crashed down on her.

She cried out, but Morana did not move her hand. After a few seconds, she pulled back, and Valerie gasped for breath.

"What did you do to me?" She asked, and Morana walked towards her throne once more.

"I bound your soul to me; if you go back on your promise, I will know." The words sent a shiver down her spine, but she nodded. The ink that had formed on her back was written in old runes, outdated even by faerie script; it curved like a snake ready to strike. Valerie did not feel afraid at that moment; she felt powerful.

History would forever remember that moment, where Valerie Denisera, Queen of Cyneria, the mortal conduit to the Goddess of Death, pledged her existence to her god, if only to take revenge on the one who had stolen her heart for himself.

Acknowledgements

Although I have written a few books, this is the first one I ever considered publishing.

I have had a love for writing since I was a young girl. Being an immigrant with few people to relate to, and even fewer to speak my native language with, I defaulted to writing. I wrote so many stories that my drawers are full of them. And yet something always stopped me from pursuing my dream of being an author. I always assumed my dreams were too far-fetched or would never come true. And yet here I am, putting this novel out there. I don't expect to gain a large fan base; I want to live with the fact that I put my work out there. Maybe if I am lucky, another young girl will be inspired to pursue her dreams.

I would like to thank a few people who have had a massive impact on my writing and on who I am as a person. Dad, I have no idea how you could survive all the things you have and still have time to help me edit my first novel. Your love for languages and literature has inspired me to pursue this dream of mine. It would not have come true without your encouragement. Carmien, I love you so much. I am so thankful to have a sister as precious as you, who fills my life with happiness, even when I feel low. You are so beautiful and a talented artist, and I hope that in writing this novel, you feel the courage to pursue your dreams, whatever they may be. Mom, I know we haven't always gotten along, but you have inspired me to never give up on my dreams and to remember that who you are at the core of your being is the most important thing to cherish.

Kate Kramer. Where do I start? You have been my best friend for a few years now and have fully believed in all my writing projects, no matter how aloof or boring. I could not be here without you. I believe you will become a well-published author, and don't worry, I will always mention you when speaking about my book. To Favour Omotoso, Emily Le, Leanne Siu, and Miss Hillier, thank you for inspiring me to write this novel. You are all such strong women in my life, and I will be eternally grateful for the impact you have made on not just my life, but my legacy. Thank you for always believing in me and carrying me through tough times, even if you didn't know it.

To Lily Brandt and Benjamin Carter, thank you for believing that my writing could be something well-crafted and even beautiful. I wish you both the best in every way possible.

I want to say that none of this would be possible without the talents God has given me to write down all these words. I give him all the glory for allowing me to pursue this storyline.

I want to thank my favourite authors (although it is unlikely they will read my work), R.F. Kuang, Sarah J. Maas, and Holly Black, for inspiring me in the most significant ways to write my novel. You have all crafted beautiful stories displaying love, loss, and what it means to think like a woman. Your novels have all changed the way women are seen in our world. I will be forever grateful that I got to read your novels.

And to everyone back home in South Africa: I miss you, I love you, and remember never to forget what your dreams can allow you to do.

Marthelize du Toit

December 2025.

www.ingramcontent.com/pod-product-compliance
Lightning Source LLC
Chambersburg PA
CBHW060259310726
48976CB00007B/2132